The ACCIDENTAL Escort

The ACCIDENTAL Escort

PATRICK C DUFFY

BIG MOOSE
PUBLISHING

ISBN: 978-1-989840-80-1(sc)
ISBN: 978-1-989840-81-8(e)
Big Moose Publishing 12/24

*For everyone who helped get me to
where I am right now*

CONTENTS

Chapter 1

LEAVING HOME

I always knew I'd leave this town. It wasn't a matter of if, just *when*. And now the moment has come. I've got a one-way ticket to London, a duffel bag slung over my shoulder, and a travel guide of England tucked under my arm. It's 1999, and the new millennium is just around the corner. While everyone else in town is worried about Y2K and the world coming to an end, I have other things on my mind—like starting fresh and making something of myself.

I'm Ciaran—Irish Catholic by birth, though I wouldn't say I've kept the faith. I grew up with all the rituals and beliefs, but as for what's waiting for us beyond this life? Who really knows. There's a whole world right here, right now, and that's what I'm focused on.

I guess I'm fairly average in the big scheme of things. I stay fit; workouts and Jiu Jitsu are a staple in my week. I don't do it for appearances—though I get by all right in that department. I do it for the discipline. I like the way it keeps my head clear and my instincts sharp. I'm on the taller side, a decent head of hair (for now, anyway), and I've been told I have a classic kind of look—whatever that means.

People say I'm liberal-minded, and I suppose that's true. Nothing really shocks me. I figure if someone wants to live a certain way, as long as they're not harming anyone, I'm the last one to judge. I'm open to pretty much anything. I think experience makes life richer, and the more we understand people's stories, the better. Besides, I'm not sure anyone has it all figured out, so there's no sense in pretending I do.

Humor is my go-to, maybe a bit sarcastic and dry, but it's just how I see the world. I'm good with my own company, but I get along with others just fine. I'm a bit of a loner by habit, maybe, but I enjoy the freedom it brings. Life has its ups and downs, but the way I see it, stay open, stay curious, and it all balances out.

After completing an undergrad degree in Saskatoon, I wasn't sure what I was going to do, and I am not ready to start a career. One of my professors told me about an Arts program focusing on literature and composition in London, England. I figured it was a long shot, but I had nothing to lose and submitted my application. Surprisingly, I was accepted. And with the small scholarship I received and help from my parents, I was able to make it work.

I haven't left Saskatoon yet, but London is already alive in my mind, an endless daydream I kept turning over whenever I walked these same familiar streets. Here, I know every brick and stretch of sidewalk like the back of my hand. There is a rhythm to life in Saskatoon, this little city in the middle of Canada. It's a rhythm that's comfortable but starts to feel like a loop you can't break. I look out over the wide, open prairies, and all I see are horizons I've already memorized. London, though—that was something else entirely.

I imagined myself stepping into a city that never seemed to sleep, every corner buzzing with strangers and stories, with accents I couldn't even place. The skyscrapers, the museums, the way the history and future seemed to collide on those narrow, crowded streets—it all felt thrilling, as though the city itself was just waiting for me to get there and jump in. I could almost hear the rush of traffic, the hum of people, that electric pulse of life that Saskatoon just didn't have. Daydreaming about London felt like I was standing on the edge of something huge and unpredictable, and that was the best part. I knew that the moment I set foot in that city, everything would be different—new, chaotic, bigger than anything I'd ever known.

***

My family stood by the truck, shifting from foot to foot, trying to figure out how to say goodbye without making it weird. Mom was the first to crack, pulling me into a bone-crushing hug.

"You're gonna call as soon as you land, right?" she said, her voice muffled into my shoulder.

"Yeah, Mom, I'll call." She didn't need to remind me—I knew the drill. Land, find a payphone, drop a couple of coins, and tell her I was still alive.

"Every Sunday, too," she added, pulling back to dab her eyes with a tissue. "You know I'll be waiting by the phone."

Dad stood nearby with his hands in his pockets, looking about as comfortable as a moose in church. "Just keep your head on straight," he grunted. "You're going there to study, not to mess around."

"Got it, Dad." The man had two emotional settings: stern advice and stern silence. This was his version of "I love you."

My little sister Maddie, eight years old and clutching her stuffed rabbit, looked up at me with wide, teary eyes. "Will you write me letters?"

"Of course I will." I gave her a reassuring smile. "And I'll even send you a postcard of Big Ben."

"Promise?"

"Promise." She hugged me tightly, like she thought

I might change my mind and stay.

James, my older brother, came next, with a smirk that said, *Don't forget you're the middle child.* He slapped me on the back so hard I stumbled. "Don't let them Brits turn you into a wimp, eh?"

"Yeah, yeah," I muttered, adjusting my duffel bag.

It was James's way of saying goodbye—tough love wrapped in sarcasm. He was staying behind to work with Dad in construction, while I was off chasing dreams in a foreign country. He never said it outright, but I knew there was a part of him that thought I was being reckless, running off to study literature and philosophy, while the rest of the family stayed grounded in reality.

I hopped into my dad's truck for the drive to the airport. Mom tried to keep the conversation going, but Dad turned up the radio just loud enough to drown out her questions. Garth Brooks crooned in the background, and Maddie fell asleep with her head on my lap, clutching her rabbit like a lifeline. I stared out the window, watching the Canadian prairie landscape blur by, wondering what London would feel like, and then I thought about Shannon Ryan. She was the only person that could possibly convince me to stay. We grew up together and were always close. Over the last few years we'd evolved from friends to friends with benefits, but it was so much more than that for me. I wanted to tell her how I felt for so long, but we were both so busy with school and I didn't want anything or anyone anchoring me to this town. I needed to get away and explore, go on an adventure, start living my life on my own terms. But last night, after a few drinks and being caught up in the excitement and anxiety of leaving, I finally decided to do something about it.

Sitting by the fire last night, with the smell of smoke and pine hanging heavy in the cool air, I couldn't stop glancing at her. She had this way of laughing, tilting her head just enough to catch the flicker of the flames in her eyes. I don't know why it hit me then—maybe because the night was ending, or maybe because we were both leaving—but suddenly, I was seeing her differently. Not just as the girl next door or young love. I knew in my heart that she was so much more to me than that, and I was so afraid of leaving without letting her know how I felt. Unfortunately, I had drank too much and was in no condition to go down this path.

I pulled her aside and kissed her passionately. And then I said it. I told her I loved her.

She stared at me incredulous, then her eyes watered and she pushed me away. I remember she called me selfish and asked me why I would put this on her now, the night before I left, when I had all the time in the world over the past few years to tell her. She even called me an asshole and told me I didn't know what love was anyway. And then she left. Not a great way to leave things, but then again, I was never great with timing.

And now I was leaving. There was no point thinking about it any longer. She was heading off to Edmonton, and I was bound for London. There would be a whole ocean between us. I felt foolish for ever saying anything in the first place.

When we finally reached the airport, Dad parked at the curb and killed the engine. "We'll be here when you get back," he said without looking at me. That was as close to an emotional send-off as I was going to get.

Mom hugged me again, squeezing harder than before. "Stay safe, Ciaran. And call the minute you get there."

"I will." I kissed her on the cheek, my stomach twisting in that weird, bittersweet way that only goodbyes can do.

Maddie, still half-asleep, mumbled, "Don't forget the postcard."

"I won't, kiddo."

James grinned as he pulled me into a one-armed hug. "Try not to embarrass us out there, eh?"

"I'll do my best."

With a final wave, I grabbed my bag and headed into the terminal. The sliding glass doors hissed shut behind me, cutting me off from the only world I'd ever known.

The airport was busy, filled with families, business travelers, and the occasional tourist with a camera dangling from their neck. I checked in at the counter, clutching my boarding pass like it was my golden ticket out of small-town life.

The hours before the flight dragged. I bought a coffee I didn't really want, flipped through a magazine I had no interest in, and kept glancing at the clock. I tried not to think about what I was leaving behind… or what I was heading toward.

When my flight was finally called, I boarded the plane and wedged myself into the middle seat, surrounded by strangers. The engines roared to life, and as the plane lifted off the ground, I watched the landscape of home shrink beneath me until it disappeared entirely.

The flight was long and restless. The in-flight movie was *The Matrix,* but I couldn't concentrate on anything except the thought of London—the city I'd been dreaming about for years. London had always felt like the ultimate destination, like the place I'd end up, even before I'd ever been there. It was a city that held this kind of intensity and history, one that had seen revolutions, artists, empires rise and fall—and all of that energy still lingers in its bones. I had looked at universities all over, but London kept pulling me in. The thought of studying there was more than just academics; it was like stepping into a real-life novel, a place that could actually challenge me, shape me in ways I probably didn't even understand.

The university itself was another story. It wasn't just some place where I'd memorize facts and write papers. The professors were known for pushing boundaries, challenging conventions, and that was exactly what I wanted—to be around people who lived for ideas, who weren't afraid to ask uncomfortable questions. There was something unapologetically bold about that, and it felt like exactly the place where I could finally dig deep into writing, into who I actually was and wanted to be.

And then, there was the draw of the city itself. London didn't seem to care who you were; it just kept going, full of different people from every corner of the world, each with their own story, their own reason for being there. It was huge, intimidating, relentless—and that made me want to be there even more. It wasn't Saskatoon, where things were familiar, where it was easy to settle into routines. In London, I'd have to keep up, be on my toes, adapt.

I think, deep down, I knew London was going to change me, shake me out of any comfort I might still have.

***

I landed in Heathrow, and the time difference hit me like a truck. Saskatoon felt worlds away, and not just because of the distance. Suddenly, it was eight hours behind me, like I'd left my body clock stuck in the middle of the prairies. But I'd made up my mind. No way was I going to let jet lag take me down on my first day. I'd just have to grit my teeth, power through, and force my internal clock to catch up.

Navigating Heathrow was a trip in itself. It was

bigger than any airport I'd seen, packed with people moving at twice the speed I was used to. After customs and wrestling with my bags, I found my way to the Tube, London's Underground, which I'd been half excited, half anxious to try. The Piccadilly Line from Heathrow into central London was packed, and everything felt so different. People were reading books in different languages, talking on phones in accents that made me feel like I was in a movie. And the landscape outside the window kept changing, from open skies near the airport to the dense sprawl of buildings that stretched on forever as we got closer to the city center.

By the time I arrived at my station, I was wiped. I felt a bit disoriented, like my brain was floating somewhere over the Atlantic. But as I finally dragged my bags up onto the street, I had my first real look at London. It was everything I'd imagined and more— these massive old buildings, pubs on every corner, and red buses darting through the streets like they had someplace crucial to be.

I grabbed a cab for the last stretch to the university, watching the streets blur past as the cabbie weaved through traffic like it was second nature. My mind was buzzing with exhaustion, but the thrill kept me awake. When we pulled up to the university, I took a deep breath. The air tinged with the mix of city exhaust, old stone, and a bit of rain. I was here. Jet-lagged to the bone and dead tired, but here. London had me, and I couldn't wait to see what was waiting around the corner.

As I rode through the bustling city, it seemed almost otherworldly. The streets were a maze of iconic red double-decker buses that wound through vibrant and eclectic neighborhoods. The storefronts glowed with modern neon lights, a stark contrast to the historic buildings that lined the streets. It was a sensory overload. Sounds of street performers and smells of diverse cuisines filled the air. This was the London of my dreams, a perfect blend of tradition and innovation that left me in awe. When we pulled up to the flat, I paid the driver with the cash I had stashed in my coat. He tipped his hat and drove off, leaving me alone in front of a building that looked older than Canada itself.

For a moment, I just stood there, gripping the handle of my duffel bag, wondering what the hell I'd gotten myself into. This was it—my new life, my new beginning. All I had to do was open the door and step inside.

I took a deep breath, adjusted the bag on my shoulder, and whispered to myself, "Here we go."

Chapter 2

PAYING THE BILLS

University life came at me with full force and at lightning speed. I had barely settled in before I found myself immersed in never-ending reading lists, large lecture halls, and intense study groups. The professors didn't guide you through the process; instead, they handed you thick books and expected you to navigate through them on your own.

I welcomed the challenge with open arms. Philosophy, history, and literature were not just mere subjects; they were gateways to new and thought-provoking ideas that I had never encountered before back in my hometown.

There was one thing the brochures didn't mention. London was expensive as hell. The rent on my student flat ate through the money I made over the summer and what my parents gave me faster than I'd anticipated, and groceries weren't far behind. I quickly learned that a diet of pasta and toast was the cheapest way to survive. Standing in front of the stove at night boiling spaghetti, I wondered if Hemingway ever had to eat like this.

So, I did what every broke student does. I looked for a job.

After a few days of scouring bulletin boards and flipping through newspapers, I found a gig as a bartender at a local pub called *The King's Arms*. The pay wasn't great, but it was close to the university, and they didn't seem to care that I was still learning how to pour a decent pint. Plus, it was cash-in-hand, which meant I could avoid the awkwardness of setting up a UK bank account.

The pub had character – wood-paneled walls, a fireplace that never seemed to light properly, and regulars who knew more about my personal life after one shift than my flatmates did after three weeks. My boss, Patrick, was a grumpy old man with a permanent scowl, but as long as I showed up on time and didn't spill too many drinks, he left me alone.

Pouring the perfect pint wasn't something I ever thought I'd need to master, but my manager, Patrick, insisted it was "an art form." After a few shifts at the pub, it didn't take long to realize just how seriously people took it around here.

"All right, lad," Patrick said, gesturing me over to the tap. "First rule of pouring a pint is it's all about patience and finesse. No one wants a rush job. Got it?"

I nodded, trying to act like I understood the significance of pouring beer at a particular angle. He grabbed a glass and held it at a 45-degree slant under the tap with the same care someone might use to handle fine glassware. His movements were so smooth and natural, like he'd done this thousands of times.

"Angle the glass like this," he explained, showing me how to keep my hand steady. "And the tap isn't just on or off. It's a soft start and a controlled stop. No one wants to drink half a glass of foam."

He nudged the lever open just slightly, and a perfect stream of amber liquid started to fill the glass. I leaned in closer, watching the foam just barely form along the edges of the glass as it filled.

"Once you're about three-quarters full, you straighten the glass up," he continued. "Let the rest fill up, and close the tap right before the foam tops out. That way, you get that perfect, creamy finish."

Patrick held up the newly poured pint. It was beautiful, really: a golden amber with a cloud of foam sitting precisely at the top.

"Your turn," he challenged, giving me a nudge.

I grabbed a glass, trying to ignore the nerves kicking in, and angled it under the tap just as he had. With one steadying breath, I eased the lever open, watching as the beer began to flow. I glanced at Patrick, who gave me a slight nod. The foam started to form gently around the edges as the liquid rose in the glass.

"Good. Keep watching," Patrick encouraged.

I waited until the glass was about three-quarters full, then carefully straightened it, aiming for that perfect balance. I shut off the tap and pulled the glass away, almost holding my breath as I studied it. The foam sat right at the top, maybe not as flawless as Patrick's, but close enough.

"Not bad," he said, giving it a look-over. "Not perfect, but you'll get there. We'll make a proper bartender out of you yet."

From that day on, I started to really enjoy the rhythm of pouring each pint. The regulars noticed too, giving nods of approval or, sometimes, an encouraging "good work" after a particularly nice pour. I could feel myself getting the hang of it, each pull from the tap smoother and more controlled.

Who'd have thought that pouring a pint could be a source of pride. But I had to admit, each time I nailed it, I felt a little more at home behind that bar.

I settled into a routine. I attended lectures during the day, worked at the pub at night, and crammed in my reading whenever I could. But it didn't take long for the cracks to show. I'd stumble into class half-asleep, missing deadlines and falling behind on my assignments. My dream of becoming a writer seemed farther away with each double shift.

Still, I told myself it was temporary. I just needed

to get through the first semester, save up a bit, and then things would ease up. But they didn't. They just seemed to get worse.

Like I said before, the reality of London's cost of living hit me like a cold slap in the face. Rent, bills, groceries—it all started piling up, fast. My savings covered tuition, but everything else was up to me, and I was burning through pay cheques just trying to keep my head above water. Every pound I earned seemed to disappear the moment it hit my account.

I'd scrounge around the house, hunting for spare change or rummaging through my drawers, sometimes finding a few coins wedged in old pockets or tossed in the back of a desk drawer. It was barely enough to stretch between the essentials. I tried to convince myself I didn't need much: plain noodles for dinner, maybe a jar of cheap sauce if I wanted to splurge. I told myself the basic stuff was all I needed. I even got used to taking sugar packets and salt shakers from work to stretch my kitchen supplies.

Then, there was rent. Every month, like clockwork, that dread would creep in, knowing my landlord expected his payment on time and that he didn't care if I had to scrape by on stale bread afterward. I was too proud to ask my parents for help, knowing they'd worry and offer whatever they could. But I'd made this decision, and I didn't want to put my family through any extra hardship. I also didn't want to give them the satisfaction of thinking I couldn't handle life on my own.

Working the late shifts at the bar was helping, but the long hours were also starting to chip away at my schoolwork. I'd spend half the night serving drinks, stumble back to my flat, try to get a few hours' sleep, and then drag myself to class the next day, barely able to focus on lectures. I was stretched thin, exhausted, and didn't see a way out. Every once in a while, I'd imagine what it'd be like to feel secure—knowing I could cover my rent without worry, or maybe afford an actual meal without counting coins.

Somehow, I kept going, surviving one day at a time, even if each day felt a bit harder than the last.

Chapter 3

THE PROPOSITION

It was now late September. I'm at work and the pub was quieter than usual. The rain was coming down hard outside, and only a few regulars huddled at the bar, nursing their drinks. I was wiping down the counter when she walked in.

She was impossible to miss—tall, elegant, and effortlessly glamorous, like she had just stepped off a movie set. With her auburn hair cascading over her shoulders and sharp, expressive features, she could've passed for Geena Davis in *Thelma & Louise*. She wore a sleek leather coat that shimmered under the dim lights, and when she smiled at me, it felt like she knew every secret I was trying to keep.

"Whiskey, neat," she said, her voice smooth and

low, with just the slightest hint of an American accent.

I poured her drink, trying not to make a fool of myself by dropping the glass. She leaned against the bar, studying me with a playful smile.

"You're not from around here, are you?"

"Nope. Canada," I said, sliding the whiskey toward her.

"Ah, a good Canadian boy." She sipped her drink, her eyes lingering on mine for a beat too long. "What brings you to London?"

"School," I answered. "University."

She gave me a look that said, *"Of course you're in university."*

"And working nights in a place like this to make ends meet," she said, as if she could read the exhaustion on my face. "Must be tough."

"It has its moments," I replied, forcing a grin.

She laughed, a low, sultry sound that made the hairs on the back of my neck stand up. "I bet it does."

For a while, we made small talk—about Canada, the miserable weather, and the quirks of British pubs. I couldn't tell if she was flirting with me or just killing time, but I enjoyed the conversation more than I wanted to admit. She had a magnetic presence, the kind that makes you forget where you are or how tired you feel.

After her second whiskey, she leaned in a little closer, resting her hand lightly on mine as I reached for her glass. "You seem like a smart young man," she said, her voice dropping to a near whisper. "Someone with ambition."

"Trying to be," I muttered, wondering where this was going.

She smiled again, a slow, knowing smile. "I like helping people like you."

There was a pause, just long enough to let the weight of her words settle between us.

"Help me how?" I asked cautiously.

Her fingers brushed over mine—just the lightest touch, but enough to send a jolt through me. "I know what it's like to struggle," she said softly. "Sometimes, a little... arrangement can make things easier. You could focus on your studies, enjoy yourself a little more. And all it takes is a bit of your time."

I blinked, trying to keep my expression neutral. "What kind of arrangement?"

Her gaze was steady, unwavering. "The kind where I pay you to spend time with me. No strings, no drama. Just fun."

The words hung in the air, and for a second, I wasn't sure if I'd heard her right.

"Are you—?"

"Yes." She tilted her head, studying me with amusement. "You're a handsome young man, Ciaran. It'd be a shame if you wore yourself out working in a place like this for pennies."

I swallowed hard, my heart racing. This was not the kind of conversation they prepared you for in small-town Saskatchewan.

"I... I don't know."

She smiled, as if she'd already made up her mind. "Think about it." She reached into her coat pocket, pulled out a sleek business card, and slid it across the bar. "If you change your mind, call me."

With that, she finished her drink, slipped the card into my hand, and gave me one last lingering look. "Take care, Ciaran."

And then she was gone, leaving behind only the scent of her perfume and the business card in my hand. I stared at it, my mind reeling.

On the card was only her name, *Andie*. And beneath it, a simple phone number.

I tucked the card into my pocket, not sure whether to laugh, panic, or run after her.

All I knew was that my life had just taken a very unexpected turn.

Chapter 4

FALLING BEHIND

The weeks that followed were a chaotic blur, each day blending into the next in a haze of exhaustion and stress. Lectures and shifts at the pub consumed my days. Sleepless nights tormented my already fragile mind. No matter how hard I tried, I couldn't keep up with the demanding pace. I would sit in my Philosophy class, surrounded by the scent of musty textbooks and the sound of scratching pencils, desperately trying to make sense of Kant's moral imperatives; but my mind was a jumbled mess, unable to comprehend even the simplest concepts.

The assigned chapters remained unread, my notes a messy scribble, and my essays were turned in late, if at all. My concentration was shot to hell, shattered by the weight of my overwhelming responsibilities. And as I struggled to keep up with the demands of my academic and work life, I could feel a heavy weight pressing down on my chest, suffocating me with its stifling grip. But worst of all were the emotions that consumed me - the frustration, the guilt, the self-doubt. I was drowning in a sea of my own failures, unable to find a way to break free. And as the days turned into weeks, I began to question if I would ever be able to find my way back to the surface.

It wasn't just the workload—it was the exhaustion. I'd get back from the pub around 2 a.m., throw myself into bed, and wake up four hours later to do it all over again. Most nights, I'd tell myself I'd stay up just a little longer to catch up on reading, but it rarely worked. I'd doze off with my textbook open in my lap, only to wake up in a panic the next morning, realizing I was even further behind.

The other students didn't seem to be struggling the way I was. They had parents who sent them care packages, money wired into their accounts when things got tight, and no need to hold down a job while juggling essays. I wasn't bitter about it—okay, maybe a little—but I knew I was on my own. Asking my parents for help still wasn't an option in my mind. They'd worked hard all their lives, and I couldn't bring myself to tell them I was drowning after only a month.

Every day felt heavier than the last, like I was

wading through quicksand. The thought of quitting my job crossed my mind more than once, but I knew that wasn't realistic. Without it, I wouldn't even be able to afford the heating bill, let alone food.

By Thanksgiving, I was cracking. My professors started pulling me aside after class to ask if everything was okay. I'd lie and tell them I was just adjusting to life in a new country. One of my tutors even suggested I go to the student support office, but what could they do? Offer me a couple of extra study hours? That wasn't going to pay my rent.

The walls of my room started closing in on me, choking me with half-finished essays, overdue assignments, and unpaid bills. I spent more time at the pub than in the library, not because I wanted to, but because I had no choice. And all the while, Andie's business card sat at the bottom of my desk drawer, like a secret too big to face.

As Thanksgiving rolled around, homesickness set in thick. I'd always been home for Thanksgiving, no exceptions. Being away from family during the holiday was something I couldn't even imagine. As I counted up my dwindling funds, I realized a flight home was entirely out of reach. I'd done the math a hundred times, searching for a miracle in my bank balance, but there was no getting around it.

Mom called one night, her voice full of excitement, and of course, it didn't take long for her to bring up Thanksgiving.

"So, have you settled in yet?" she asked, her usual warmth filling the line. "We miss you so much, honey. It's not the same without you here."

I hesitated, my mind racing through all the excuses I could give. But she knew me too well, heard the pause and sighed.

"Ciaran… listen, your dad and I talked about it. We'd be happy to help with your ticket for Christmas if that's the problem. You just have to say the word."

For a split second, I considered saying yes. But the thought of them scraping together the money—money they didn't have to spare—just to bring me back didn't sit right. I'd made this choice to be here, and I wanted to handle it on my own, even if it meant staying put.

"Thanks, Mom," I said, doing my best to keep my voice light. "But I'll figure it out. I'm working some extra shifts at the pub. I'll save up."

"Are you sure?" she asked, clearly unconvinced. "We don't mind. It's just one flight, Ciaran."

"I'm sure," I replied, hating myself a bit for lying. "Besides, I could use the extra work experience. It'll be fine. Maybe I can save up enough by next year to come back for good." After we hung up, the silence in my flat felt heavier than ever.

The holiday decorations around town only made it worse—a constant reminder of everything I was missing. I threw myself into work at the pub, taking on every extra shift they'd give me, even if it meant dragging myself home in the dead of night, exhausted and wondering if any of this was worth it.

Thanksgiving dinner rolled around, and I tried to ignore the ache that came with knowing my family would be together without me. I'd told Mom I'd call when they were all gathered, but I could already feel the lump forming in my throat. It wasn't the same—nowhere close—but I'd made my decision. I had to live with it.

I made the call. I was hoping the familiar voices would help, but hearing my family all together only drove the knife deeper. They were playing games, laughing, Dad cracking his usual jokes, Mom reminding everyone to wait until after dinner to start on dessert. I could practically smell the coffee, the cinnamon rolls, the decorations my little sister put up that were always lopsided. I'd put on a cheerful front for them, promised I was doing fine, told them to eat extra stuffing for me. Then I hung up, feeling more alone than ever.

That night a feeling crept up on me with a kind of emptiness I hadn't anticipated. I thought I'd keep busy, maybe go for a walk or even read a bit to pass the time, but none of it filled the quiet. The streets outside my flat were deserted, the shops closed, even the pub down the street had its doors shut. London was just… silent… and the quiet made the loneliness louder.

I couldn't take it anymore. I poured myself a drink—then another. Music played softly on the radio, but instead of making me feel more thankful for the opportunity to be in an amazing city going to university and pursuing my dream, it just reminded me how far I was from home. I tried watching TV, scrolling through the channels until I landed on some holiday special, but it didn't hold my attention. The silence, the empty flat, the weird itch of wanting to feel something, anything other than what I was feeling— it all began to weigh down on me.

Without even thinking, I reached over to my desk drawer, yanked it open, and pulled out the card. *Andie.* Her name stared back at me, elegant and simple, above the phone number I hadn't dared to dial.

I sat there for what felt like an eternity, my thumb hovering over the numbers on my cheap Nokia phone. I told myself I wouldn't actually call. I was just holding the phone. No harm in that, right?

But then, before I could stop myself, I punched in the number and pressed the green send button.

The phone rang twice before her voice came through, smooth and familiar. "Hello?"

I froze for a second, heart pounding. "Hi, uh... It's Ciaran. From The King's Arms?"

There was a pause, followed by a warm chuckle. "Ciaran. I was starting to wonder if you'd ever call."

I let out a shaky breath, trying to keep my voice steady. "Yeah, well... I guess I'm calling now."

"I'm glad you did," she said, and I could hear the smile in her voice. "Have you thought about my offer?"

I swallowed hard, gripping the phone tighter. "Yeah. I... I think I'd like to take you up on it."

"Good." Her tone was easy, like this was the most natural conversation in the world. "I promise, you won't regret it. How about we meet tomorrow night? We can get dinner, talk a little more, and see how things go."

"Okay," I whispered, feeling like I'd just stepped off a cliff.

"I'll text you the address," she said, her voice as smooth as silk.

"Wait—uh, I don't have texting on my phone."

There was a pause, then another soft laugh. "Of course. How very 1999 of you."

She gave me the address instead—some swanky restaurant in the West End that I could barely pronounce.

"See you at 8?"

"Yeah. I'll be there."

"Goodnight, Ciaran."

"Goodnight."

I hung up the phone and sat there in stunned silence, the reality of what I'd just done settling over me like a heavy blanket.

Tomorrow night, I was going to meet Andie. And everything after that? Well, I had no idea where it would lead.

Chapter 5

DINNER WITH ANDIE

The next evening, I stood outside the restaurant, trying not to look like a lost tourist. The place was the kind of establishment that didn't have a name on the door—just sleek black walls, a brass handle, and the faint aroma of money. I caught a glimpse of myself in the reflection: damp hair from the drizzle, jacket a little too tight, and shoes that were scuffed despite my best attempt to polish them.

"You've got this," I whispered to myself, inhaling the sharp London air. "You're sophisticated. You're mature. You're Ciaran Doyle, international man of mystery."

With that pep talk out of the way, I pushed open the door and stepped inside.

The restaurant was dimly lit, with soft jazz playing in the background and tables spaced far enough apart to allow for hushed conversations. Everything about it whispered exclusive. A waiter led me to a small table in the corner, where Andie was already waiting.

She looked incredible. Her auburn hair framed her face perfectly, and her outfit—a black dress that hugged her figure—seemed both effortless and carefully chosen. She gave me that same slow, knowing smile as I approached.

"Right on time," she said, crossing her legs.

I tried not to trip over the chair as I sat down. "Of course. Punctuality is... you know, important." *Good start, Ciaran. Very smooth.*

The waiter came by, and Andie ordered a bottle of wine without even glancing at the menu. I tried to act cool, but my knowledge of wine was limited to whatever Patrick at the pub kept behind the bar.

The wine arrived, and Andie swirled her glass like she'd been born doing it. I copied her, though I had no idea what I was supposed to be looking for. When I took a sip, it tasted... like wine.

"Good, isn't it?" Andie said with a playful smirk, watching me carefully.

"Yeah, very... complex?" I nodded like a connoisseur, hoping she wouldn't ask me to elaborate.

She laughed, a soft, knowing sound that made my skin prickle. "You're adorable."

I nearly choked on my drink. "Thanks," I

mumbled, not entirely sure if it was a compliment or an observation.

As the night went on, I tried my best to seem worldly, which mostly involved nodding along whenever Andie talked about her business ventures. Something to do with marketing or consulting—I couldn't keep track, but she seemed important. Every now and then, she'd throw me a curveball of a question.

"So, what do you study again?" she asked.

"History, philosophy, that kind of thing," I said, trying to sound casual. "You know, just... studying the world. Thinking big thoughts."

She arched an eyebrow. "Ah, a philosopher. Do you think a philosopher can also be... a good lover?"

My brain short-circuited. "I, uh, well... Socrates never really covered that, but I think it's definitely... possible."

She smiled as if she knew exactly how uncomfortable I was and found it charming. "We'll see," she murmured, taking another sip of wine.

I wasn't sure if I wanted to pass out or cheer. This woman was playing me like a violin, and I was loving every second of it. But beneath the excitement, a knot of anxiety sat in my stomach. Could I really go through with this? Was this the kind of thing good-natured boys from small-town Canada were supposed to do?

The answer came when Andie leaned in, her lips brushing my ear as she whispered, "Why don't we skip dessert and go back to my place?"

My heart felt like it might burst out of my chest. I nodded, muttering something that was probably meant to sound suave but came out as a strangled, "Yeah. Sure."

*****

Andie's apartment was everything I expected: sleek, modern, and filled with expensive furniture that looked like it belonged in a magazine. I stood awkwardly by the door as she slipped off her heels, moving through the space with the easy confidence of someone who knew exactly what she wanted.

"Relax, Ciaran." She gave me a playful look. "You look like you've never done this before."

I laughed nervously. "Maybe not with, uh… someone as experienced as you."

She raised an eyebrow, clearly amused. "Let's make sure you don't disappoint."

She walked over, so close I could smell the faint perfume on her skin. With a gentle push, she guided me to the couch, straddling me effortlessly. My heart raced as she leaned in, her lips brushing against mine.

"First rule," she whispered. "Confidence. If you want a woman, act like it. No hesitation."

I swallowed hard. "Right. No hesitation."

She smiled against my lips. "Good boy."

Her kiss was slow and deliberate, teasing me into submission. When I tried to speed things up, she pulled back with a knowing smirk.

"Not so fast," she murmured. "Anticipation is everything. Make her want more."

She took my hand and placed it on her thigh, guiding me with the patience of a teacher. "Explore. Take your time. Women love to feel desired. Show her that you're not in a rush to get to the finish line."

I followed her lead, my hands tracing the curves of her body as she whispered instructions in my ear. "Gentle at first, then build. Make her wonder what's coming next."

She showed me how to read the little signs—a quickened breath, the way her muscles tensed under my touch. "Pay attention," she said softly. "Every woman is different. Learn her rhythm."

It was overwhelming and intoxicating, like learning a new language through touch. Andie was patient but firm, guiding me through every step with a combination of encouragement and playful teasing.

When I fumbled, because of course I did, she just laughed, brushing it off with a kiss. "Relax, Ciaran. This isn't an exam. It's supposed to be fun."

And it was. Somewhere between the nervousness and excitement, I found myself letting go, following her lead, but also discovering my own confidence.

By the time we finally made it to the bedroom, I wasn't just following instructions anymore. I was learning how to take control, how to give as much as I received. Andie's approval was addictive, her soft murmurs of "Yes, just like that" spurring me on.

And when it was over, when we lay tangled in the sheets, breathless and satisfied, she gave me a lazy, satisfied smile.

"You're a quick learner," she whispered, brushing a strand of hair from my face.

I grinned, still trying to catch my breath. "You're a good teacher."

She laughed softly, her fingers tracing patterns on my chest. "I think we'll have a lot of fun together, Ciaran."

And just like that, my strange new adventure had officially begun.

Chapter 6

A NEW ARRANGEMENT

I woke up the next morning to the soft light filtering through the curtains and the warm scent of coffee wafting through the air. For a moment, I lay there, eyes closed, savoring the remnants of last night's adventure.

But then it occurred to me… I was in Andie's apartment. I blinked awake and turned to find her in the kitchen, pouring steaming mugs of coffee. She looked effortlessly beautiful, her hair tousled but framing her face perfectly as she hummed to herself, lost in her own world.

I sat up, pulling the covers around me like a shield. "Uh, good morning," I called, trying to keep my voice steady.

She turned, her eyes lighting up as she set the

coffee down on the table. "Morning, sleepyhead! I hope you like it black—made it just for you."

My stomach twisted with a mix of embarrassment and excitement. "Thanks. I appreciate it."

As I swung my legs over the side of the bed, I felt that familiar rush of anxiety. I'd spent the night with this stunning woman, and now she was brewing coffee for me like we were an old couple. What on earth had I gotten myself into?

Andie slid into the chair across from me, her expression thoughtful as she watched me sip the coffee. "So, what did you think of last night?"

I choked a little on the coffee. "Um, well... it was definitely... an experience."

She laughed, a light, melodic sound that eased some of my tension. "Just an experience? I thought you were quite the natural."

My cheeks flushed. "You're a great teacher."

Her gaze softened, and she leaned in, resting her chin on her hand. "You know, I'm genuinely impressed. You have potential, Ciaran."

"Potential?" I repeated, confused. I didn't know if she meant potential in the bedroom or something more.

"Yes," she said, a playful glint in her eye. "I see a lot of possibilities for you. Have you ever thought about making this arrangement a bit more official?"

I cocked my head, trying to decipher what she meant. "Official?"

"Let's not beat around the bush. I'm talking about a business plan."

My eyebrows shot up. "A business plan? For what?"

"For your new line of work, of course! You have the skills, and I know how to market them. Think of it as a mutually beneficial partnership."

I stared at her, still trying to process the idea. "You want to help me become... an escort?"

"Exactly!" she said, her enthusiasm infectious. "You provide your services, and I'll help you find clients. Think of it like a business relationship."

I ran a hand through my hair, a rush of thoughts swirling in my mind. "But... I don't know how to do that. What if no one wants to hire me?"

Andie laughed again, shaking her head as if I were being ridiculous. "Ciaran, you underestimate yourself. You're charming, handsome, and you already have experience, thanks to last night. Trust me; I can help you find customers."

I shifted in my chair, a mix of excitement and anxiety bubbling up. "And in exchange, you want... what exactly?"

"Just what we agreed upon." She raised her eyebrows suggestively. "We keep having fun, and I help you with the business side. It's win-win!"

I took a deep breath, feeling a rush of adrenaline. The thought of turning my awkward situation into a legitimate business was both terrifying and thrilling. "What kind of customers are we talking about?"

"Oh, a variety. Professional women, likely—business types who want companionship, someone fun, and attractive without the complications of a relationship." She winked. "Think of it like a service. You're not just an escort; you're providing a unique experience."

My pulse quickened as I imagined it. The thought of being paid for my time was mind-blowing. "But what if I mess up?"

Andie leaned forward, her expression earnest. "You won't. I'll teach you everything you need to know. We'll create a profile for you, set some ground rules, and then I'll help you network. It'll be like my own little project."

I ran my fingers along the edge of the table, grappling with the implications. "And I'll still see you?"

"Of course!" she said, her voice smooth as silk. "I wouldn't want you to forget your most important client."

I chuckled nervously, the tension easing slightly. "So, where do we start?"

She grinned, clearly pleased. "First, we need a name. Something catchy that will grab attention."

"A name?" I echoed, biting my lip. "Like what?"

"Something fun, sexy, and memorable. How about 'Ciaran the Luscious'?"

I snorted, nearly spilling my coffee. "Definitely not that."

She laughed, her eyes sparkling with mischief. "Alright, let's brainstorm. You want it to be appealing, right? What about 'Daring Doyle'? Or 'Lusty Ciaran'?"

I groaned, covering my face with my hands. "You're killing me."

"Just trying to help!" she said, still chuckling.

As the banter continued, I felt a strange sense of camaraderie building between us. Sure, I was navigating uncharted waters, but if Andie was going to guide me, maybe I could turn this peculiar situation into something I'd never imagined possible.

"Okay, how about 'Ciaran the Charmer'?" I suggested finally, looking up at her.

She clapped her hands together, clearly excited. "I love it! We can work with that. Now, let's get started!"

Chapter 7

FIRST IMPRESSIONS (AND A BICYCLE)

I stared at the ceiling of my tiny apartment, clutching my ancient flip phone. Andie's voice message had been short and to the point:

"Got your first client. Be at her flat by 8 tonight. Don't screw this up. Good luck!"

It was 7:15.

I jumped up, glancing at the clock and muttering curses as I pulled on the only pair of dress pants I owned—charcoal gray, a little too tight around the thighs. They were left over from my high school prom and still smelled faintly of mothballs. I grabbed a white button-down shirt, tugged it on, and then checked myself in the mirror.

"Okay, Ciaran ol' boy," I muttered, slapping my cheeks lightly for motivation. "You got this. You're charming. Mature. You are a *professional*."

I was sitting there, my hands drumming on the edge of the bed, feeling a strange mix of excitement and dread washing over me. My first client was minutes away, and no amount of preparation or rehearsed lines in my head had calmed me down. The nervous energy was all-consuming, and I could feel it coiled in my stomach, tense, like I was about to step into a ring for a fight I hadn't trained for. I'd told myself over and over that this was just another kind of work, that people did stranger things for money every day. Still, the thought of it made me feel... exposed, vulnerable even.

Beyond the nerves, there was the moral tugging I hadn't really expected. This was more than just a job. There was a part of me—the part that was raised on family dinners, Sunday mass, and a thousand reminders about "right and wrong"—that was still questioning if this was something I should even be doing. Could I really go through with it? Was this a line I should cross? It wasn't so much guilt as it was uncertainty, a question of whether this decision would change something fundamental in me, something I might not be able to come back from.

But in the end, it was curiosity that tipped the scale. My life had always been a little too predictable, and here was a chance to break the mold, to see who

I was without the boundaries I'd always accepted without question. I wanted to know if I could do this, if I had it in me to face the unknown and meet it head-on without apology. I took a deep breath, feeling the pounding of my heart as I glanced at the clock, and told myself it was time. Time to find out if this was something I was actually capable of, or if the nerves and the doubts would get the better of me.

The plan was simple: get to the woman's place, keep things polite, and follow her lead. It couldn't be that hard, right?

Except now there was a problem: the Tube was delayed, and my budget didn't exactly cover cab fare. That left me with only one option: my bike.

I glanced down at my dress pants with a groan, tucking the right pant leg into my sock. No way was I going to show up to my first gig covered in chain grease.

"This is fine," I kept repeating trying to convince myself, as I began pedaling my bike down the street. "Sophisticated. Elegant. Every gentleman arrives to his first date by bicycle."

At exactly 8:03 p.m., I arrived at the woman's flat, slightly out of breath from the ride. I double-checked the crumpled paper with the address Andie had given me, then leaned my bike against the wall next to her door.

After a deep breath, I rang the buzzer.

The door clicked open, and I stepped into a

modest but tastefully decorated apartment. Adjusting the pant leg I'd tucked into my sock, I looked up just as the woman appeared in the doorway.

She was older than I'd expected—mid-50s, maybe. Tall, slender, with a chic bob of silver-blonde hair and freshly applied red lipstick. She wore a fitted black dress, and her eyes sparkled with a mix of amusement and intrigue as they scanned me up and down.

"Well, aren't you something," she said, her lips curling into a half-smile.

I cleared my throat, suddenly feeling ridiculous standing there with my bike helmet under one arm and a slightly wrinkled dress shirt. "Sorry, Tube issues," I blurted. "Had to bike here."

She raised an eyebrow. "I see that. And the sock? Very… practical."

I winced and quickly yanked my pant leg out of my sock, offering a sheepish grin. "Yeah, didn't want to get grease on the pants. You know how it is."

She laughed, a soft, throaty sound that immediately eased my nerves. "Smart boy. Come in, then. I'm Elise." She handed me an envelope saying "This is for you. Now that we've got the business side of things out of the way, let's begin enjoying the evening."

Elise poured two glasses of wine and handed one to me. I was grateful for something to steady my nerves and took a sip, glancing around her apartment. The place was tastefully decorated, with framed black-and-white photos lining the walls and soft jazz floating from a record player in the corner.

"So, how long have you been doing this?" she asked, settling onto the sofa with her wine.

"Oh, uh… this is actually my first time," I admitted, scratching the back of my neck.

Elise smiled knowingly. "A virgin, then. How charming."

I nearly choked on my wine. "I wouldn't exactly say that—"

"I mean professionally," she interrupted, her grin widening.

"Right, professionally," I mumbled, feeling the heat rise to my face.

She leaned forward, crossing her legs with such smooth elegance that it made me acutely aware of how out of my depth I really was. "Relax, darling. You're doing fine so far."

I exhaled a breath I hadn't realized I was holding. "Thanks. I guess I just didn't know what to expect."

"Well, here's the thing," she said, swirling her wine. "Older women—we don't have time for games. We know what we want, and we appreciate men who can follow our lead. Think of it like a dance. You follow; I lead."

I nodded slowly, finding comfort in her directness. "That actually makes sense."

"Good. Now, let's talk business."

She patted the spot next to her on the sofa, and after a second's hesitation, I joined her. The wine was taking effect, loosening my nerves, and her confidence was contagious.

"So, here's the deal," Elise said, setting her glass on the table. "We spend the evening together. You make me feel good—mentally, physically, whatever I need. No awkwardness, no hesitation. Just two adults having a good time."

I tried to ignore my racing heart. "And… how will I know if I'm doing it right?"

Elise smiled, a mischievous glint in her eye. "Oh, trust me. You'll know."

She leaned in, her perfume—a mix of jasmine and citrus—filled my senses. "The key is to relax. Enjoy yourself. You might just find you're better at this than you think."

I swallowed hard, but managed a grin. "So… no pressure, then?"

Elise laughed, a warm, infectious sound that immediately put me at ease. "Exactly. Now, let's see if that charming smile of yours is good for more than just conversation."

To my surprise, the night wasn't nearly as awkward as I'd feared. Elise was patient and calm, but also wonderfully direct, guiding me with the ease of someone who knew exactly what she wanted. It was like she'd tapped into a quiet confidence in me that I didn't even know was there. I followed her lead, and it all began to feel natural, even… effortless.

In fact, I realized I was actually enjoying myself.

There was something undeniably refreshing about being with a woman who didn't dance around her desires, who knew exactly what she wanted and wasn't afraid to say it out loud. She led every moment, from the first sip of wine to the subtle cues she dropped along the way, and for the first time in a long time, I wasn't second-guessing myself or trying to read between the lines. It was simple, almost instinctual.

When I finally left her apartment—helmet in hand, and pant leg tucked into my sock to avoid the bike chain—I felt a strange, undeniable sense of accomplishment. I pedaled home through the quiet, dimly lit streets of London, feeling lighter than I had in weeks. I couldn't keep the grin from spreading across my face.

I didn't open the envelope right away, because I thought it would make me look cheap, so I waited until I was home. I closed the apartment door behind me, the faint squeak of the hinge echoing in the quiet space. I sat on the edge of my bed, the mattress creaking beneath me, and stared at the crisp white paper like it might burn me if I opened it. When I finally tore it open, the sight of seven neatly folded €100 bills made my stomach twist. Seven hundred euros. For a few hours of... well, fun? I guess. My heart thudded, a strange mix of shame and exhilaration. I'd never earned that much in a week, let alone in a single evening. Groceries, rent, maybe even a bit extra for books—all in my hand.

Maybe this business wasn't going to be so bad after all.

55

Chapter 8

TEDDY BEAR TROUBLE

ndie had called me the previous evening to let me know about another appointment, and I woke up to a flurry of nervous energy. I'd spent the night tossing and turning, half-excited, half-terrified about what lay ahead. Andie had set me up with a client named Geena, who was described as "a lovely woman with a unique sense of adventure."

But here's the kicker: Geena had a *thing* for stuffed animals. As in, she wanted me to wear a teddy bear costume while we... you know.

I had laughed nervously when Andie mentioned it, thinking she was joking. But she wasn't. "Trust me, Ciaran," she said with that confident smile. "Geena is going to be a great client. Just be yourself...in a bear suit."

So, there I was, standing in front of my closet, trying to suppress my panic as I prepared for the absurdity of the day ahead. I had the costume on my mind, but first, I needed to acquire it.

After some extensive Googling (or, as extensive as 1999 dial-up internet could manage), I found a local costume shop that promised to have "everything you could ever want." As I walked down the street, my heart raced at the thought of trying on a full-body bear suit in public. *What if someone I knew saw me?*

The shop was filled with an eclectic mix of costumes, wigs, and props. The smell of plastic and cheap fabric wafted through the air as I made my way to the back, where I found it: a giant, fuzzy teddy bear costume that looked as if it had seen far too many children's parties.

"Excuse me," I said to the shop owner, who was a burly man with a thick mustache. "I'd like to try this on."

The man looked at me with a knowing grin, as if he had seen every sort of costume request in the world. "Sure thing, kid. Just take it in the changing room over there."

I hesitated, then nodded, trying to maintain my composure as I took the costume. Inside the changing room, I faced the daunting task of donning it. The suit was bulky and warm, and I quickly realized it was a little more difficult than I anticipated. After struggling for a few moments, I finally managed to wriggle into the fluffy monstrosity, complete with oversized bear ears and a plastic nose that felt ridiculously silly.

I stood in front of the mirror, trying to take myself seriously, but all I could see was a ridiculous teddy bear staring back at me. I turned from side to side, and that's when I realized—it was also quite tight.

"Okay, bear boy," I muttered to myself. "Time to own it."

With a deep breath, I stepped out of the changing room, my heart pounding. "How does it look?" I asked the shop owner, who barely held back a laugh.

"Perfect!" he said, wiping away a tear of laughter. "You're ready for a picnic, kid."

"Thanks?" I replied, trying to gauge if he was being sincere or just mocking me. I paid for the costume, feeling a little lighter in my wallet and much heavier in fluff.

Once I got home, I realized I had to make some adjustments. After all, I couldn't just wear the costume as-is; that would be absurd. So, with some scissors, a needle, and a lot of hope, I altered the suit. I snipped at the seams to make it more breathable and dug out some old black sweatpants to wear underneath for comfort.

When I finished, I stood back and admired my handiwork. "Not bad, Ciaran. Not bad at all," I muttered, feeling a surge of confidence. *Who knew I had such a flair for costume design?*

***

Later that evening, I found myself pacing in my room, the costume crammed in a bag and ready to go. I glanced at the clock, my nerves spiking as I realized it was time to leave. I headed to Geena's place.

I knocked, and the door swung open to reveal Geena, who looked lovely in her own right. She was in her early thirties, with a soft, pretty face and a warm, easy smile that lit up the room. She was a little on the heavier side, with curves that suited her well, and her black hair was pulled back in a casual ponytail that gave her a friendly, approachable look. As soon as I walked in, I noticed two things. First, the apartment was swanky, and filled with art that I couldn't quite understand. Second, was Geena's energy—a kind of bubbly, almost giddy excitement that made her seem both nervous and thrilled to be here.

"You made it!" She laughed easily, her eyes darting around the room and then settling back on me, as if she was as curious about this encounter as I was. There was a sweetness to her that put me at ease, even as I was still working through my own nerves. "Uh, yeah," I said, trying not to stammer as I stepped inside. "Thanks for having me."

"I can't wait to see you in the costume!" she said, practically bouncing on her toes.

The moment of truth had arrived. I grinned nervously, "Well, I guess it's time to bring out my inner bear."

I headed to the bathroom to change, feeling the weight of the world on my shoulders. After all, it's not every day a guy finds himself dressing up like a stuffed animal for a date.

I slipped into the costume, adjusting the fuzzy fabric and trying to figure out how to maneuver without tripping. With a deep breath, I opened the bathroom door and stepped out.

"Ta-da!" I announced, striking a pose.

Geena's eyes lit up, and she burst into laughter, her delight making my heart race. "You look incredible! Absolutely adorable!"

I tried to keep a straight face, but the ridiculousness of the situation began to hit me. "I feel like a big, furry marshmallow," I said, attempting to sound confident.

"Exactly what I wanted!" she said, clapping her hands together. "Now, come here and let's get started."

We settled onto the couch, and Geena couldn't contain her excitement as she pulled out an assortment of stuffed animals—each one carefully arranged like a miniature audience. "These are my friends," she said with a grin. "They'll help set the mood."

I glanced at the plush toys and stifled a laugh. *This was truly absurd.*

"Okay, Mr. Bear," Geena said, her tone playful. "Let's have some fun!"

As I awkwardly embraced the role of *Teddy Bear*, I found myself slipping into character. I bumbled around, doing exaggerated bear-like movements, growling softly, and trying to keep the atmosphere light. Geena was in stitches, laughing so hard that I almost forgot how strange it was.

"Wow, I didn't know a bear could be so charming!" she teased, her laughter infectious.

I found myself leaning into the absurdity, playing up my inner teddy. The performance felt oddly liberating as I shifted from nerves to sheer joy. It wasn't long before Geena was urging me to "dance" with her stuffed animals, and I complied, flailing my arms in the most bear-like way I could muster.

It was ridiculous. It was wild. And somehow, I was having the time of my life.

When the dance came to an end, I found myself inching closer to Geena, leaning in for a kiss as she giggled. She pulled me close, her lips brushing against the plush fabric of the costume. "You're definitely the best teddy bear I've ever met," she said, her voice low and teasing.

Geena sauntered toward me, her silk robe parting just enough to reveal smooth, pale skin and a black lace bra underneath. She was watching me with a glint of playful mischief, and I could feel myself blushing beneath the massive teddy bear head.

"You won't be in there for too long, darling," she purred, trailing a finger down the fuzzy chest of the costume. "Just long enough to get me... in the mood."

I cleared my throat, feeling both ridiculous and strangely intrigued. "So, uh... how does this work exactly?" I asked, my voice muffled from inside the bear head.

She grinned, an almost predatory gleam in her eye. "We cuddle, like a good teddy bear would. And once I'm ready…" She gave me a wink that made my heart race despite the absurdity. "Then the fun really begins."

I let out a half-laugh, half-sigh of disbelief and shuffled over to the bed, where Geena was already sprawled across the pillows, looking every bit the queen of her castle. She patted the space beside her. "Come on, big guy. Don't be shy."

With a final groan, I climbed onto the bed, feeling the plush suit squeak and rustle as I adjusted myself. She leaned in close, nestling against my fluffy shoulder, and somehow, I found myself relaxing a little. There was something oddly comforting about the absurdity of the moment.

Geena giggled like a schoolgirl. "Oh, this is perfect. Just what I needed."

She wrapped her arms around my plush midsection, sighing contentedly. "Mmm, you're such a good teddy…"

I lay there stiffly in the costume, unsure of how to proceed. "Is there, uh, anything specific the teddy should be doing?" I asked, my voice still muffled.

"Shhh," Geena whispered, pressing a finger to the bear's fuzzy snout. "Just cuddle. That's all you need to do."

So, I cuddled.

It felt surreal—lying there in this giant bear suit, holding a nearly naked woman who sighed and murmured happily in my arms. Yet, it wasn't as awkward as I'd anticipated. There was something oddly intimate about the moment, like being let into a secret corner of someone's world. Her warmth seeped through the costume, and I could feel the tension of the day melting away as we settled into this absurd yet surprisingly comforting scenario.

After a few minutes, Geena whispered, "Okay, Teddy. Time to take this off now."

A part of me felt a mix of relief and reluctance. It was an unexpected pleasure to be her cuddly companion, even if I did look utterly ridiculous. But as I began to pull off the head of the suit, I wondered what kind of fun might await us next.

I peeled off the bear head, gasping for air as my sweaty face finally emerged into the cool air. "God, it's like a sauna in there," I said, trying to shake off the lingering heat.

Geena laughed, her eyes sparkling with mischief. "Poor thing. Let me help."

She moved closer, reaching for the zipper on my back. As she slowly and sensually pulled it down, I could feel the fabric sliding off my shoulders, and my heart raced with a mix of anticipation and exhilaration. When the suit finally fell away, it revealed my bare chest beneath, and I couldn't help but feel a little exposed.

Her playful smile shifted to something deeper, more appreciative, as her hands explored the contours of my muscles. "Well, well… under all that fluff, you really are quite a treat, aren't you?" Her voice was a sultry whisper, and the heat in her gaze sent a thrill down my spine.

I grinned, feeling my nerves dissolve under her scrutiny as her touch became more insistent. Geena's fingers traced the lines of my body, igniting a fire within me. There was a boldness in her movements, an enthusiasm that was both exciting and slightly overwhelming. She leaned closer, her breath warm against my skin, and I could sense her eagerness.

"Now that's more like it," she purred, her fingers dancing across my chest. I could feel her hunger, the way her body shifted closer to mine, as if she couldn't get enough. "You're going to have to keep up with me, darling."

The way she said it, full of playful challenge, made my heart race even faster. There was no doubt about it; Geena was ready to take charge, and I was more than willing to let her. As she pulled me toward her, I felt a surge of confidence mingling with desire, eager to explore where this night would lead.

Geena guided me down onto the bed, her kisses trailing along my neck and shoulders, each touch sending a shiver through me. There was no pretension, no awkward fumbling—just an unspoken understanding. She knew exactly what she wanted, and I found myself lost in the simplicity of it, reveling in the moment.

We moved together with an easy rhythm, her soft moans mingling with my low sighs, creating a melody that felt intimate and electric. There was something undeniably sensual about the way she moved, her playful energy making me feel both desired and relaxed. It was as if we were dancing in a world all our own, where nothing else mattered, but this connection we were building.

When we finally reached that blissful end, she lay back with a satisfied sigh, her fingers gliding through my damp hair, grounding me. "You, my dear, are a natural," she said, her voice a warm caress.

I chuckled, my heart still racing. "Well, thank you. I aim to please."

Geena met my gaze with a sly smile that sent a thrill through me. "You certainly do. And I have a feeling this is the start of a very… profitable relationship."

I grinned back at her, fully aware that the delightful absurdity of this first encounter was just the beginning of many more to come. In that moment, I felt a warmth spread through me, knowing we were both in for an adventure that would blur the lines between pleasure and intimacy.

Chapter 9

THE PERKS OF BEING A BOY TOY

As the weeks rolled by, I found myself swept up in a whirlwind of surprises. My little escapade into the world of escorting had blossomed into something I could never have anticipated. I was no longer just Ciaran, the awkward college student struggling to make ends meet; I was Ciaran, the charming bear—and so much more.

Andie had been right: my unique clientele was growing, and each encounter was more ridiculous yet fulfilling than the last. With each gig, I added another skill to my belt—or, sometimes, another costume in my closet. The laughter and joy I brought to my clients became my own source of happiness. I started to see the humor in the absurdity of it all, and that made me feel more confident and alive.

But it wasn't just about the fun. The financial benefits were incredible. With each job, I was earning more than I ever thought possible. I could finally relax and enjoy life a little instead of constantly worrying about my bills and student loans. I was able to treat myself to nice meals, buy new books for my classes, and even set aside some money for a weekend getaway with friends. The weight of financial stress was slowly lifting, and it felt liberating.

My grades were improving, too. The extra income allowed me to cut back on my part-time job, which had previously consumed so much of my time and energy. I found that with fewer hours spent at work, I could dedicate more time to my studies. My focus sharpened, and I began to enjoy my classes more than I had in the past. I was diving into my coursework, and my grades reflected that newfound passion and dedication. I could feel my confidence growing, both in and out of the classroom.

Everything was looking up for me. The combination of financial stability and academic success had sparked a sense of optimism I hadn't felt in a long time. I was no longer just getting by; I was thriving. I had turned my life around, and each day felt like a new opportunity waiting to unfold. As I moved forward in this unexpected journey, I couldn't help but feel excited about what was to come. The world felt like it was filled with possibilities, and I was ready to embrace them all.

Andie had a knack for connecting people, and it didn't take long for her to create a steady stream of clients for me. At first, I had no idea how she did it; I just knew I had a full calendar and a new network forming almost overnight. But as time went on, I saw that Andie had built a web of connections through her social circles, her old clients, and her friends in elite circles.

Andie was well-connected, moving easily in high society. She attended exclusive parties and private events, always dressed in a way that turned heads and drew people in. Through quiet conversations and subtle hints, she would bring me up—a talented, young companion who could entertain, charm, and bring a little spark to their lives. These weren't just random people; they were individuals she trusted, who knew the rules of discretion, and who understood exactly what kind of arrangement they were stepping into. She never oversold me but left just enough mystery to make people curious.

Word of mouth began to spread, and once the door was open, clients started referring others. Andie was careful to keep a sense of exclusivity, vetting each client before introducing us. I realized quickly that this was part of her skill: keeping her clients feeling like they were in on a well-kept secret.

Each introduction felt casual, but precise. Andie

would invite me to events and introduce me subtly, always positioning me in ways that allowed the client to feel like they were "discovering" me. By the time our arrangement was rolling smoothly, her contacts had provided me with a steady stream of high-end clients from all walks of life—people who appreciated discretion, charisma, and a sense of fun without complication. It wasn't just business; it was an art form. And Andie was a master at work.

My phone buzzed constantly with new requests, each client so different than the last. I had moved beyond just Geena and her love for stuffed animals. There was Lucy, who wanted me to dress up as a pirate while she lounged in her hot tub, and Claire, who had a fascination with gardening and insisted on conducting a "plant-themed" date.

Despite the absurdity, I found myself laughing more than I ever had. The income was incredible. After just a month, I could finally breathe easy. I paid my rent without having to stretch my budget, which was a relief. I even managed to lease a shiny new Vespa, a sleek little number that made me feel like a million bucks whenever I hopped on the seat and grabbed the handlebars.

In the heart of London, I parked my new Vespa outside the bar where I still worked part-time. One of my coworkers, Max, eyed it with a mix of envy and disbelief. "You're telling me you can afford that now? You must be doing well for yourself."

"Oh, you know," I said with a casual shrug, trying not to let on how dramatically my life had changed. "Just a few lucky breaks."

And it didn't stop there. I tackled my school debts with the same determination I had when I first arrived in London. With each gig, I saw the balance dwindle, and I couldn't help but grin. I even paid off my student loans a semester earlier than expected.

"Look at you, the savvy businessman!" Andie teased one day as we sat in her favorite café, sipping lattes. She had whisked me away for a "business meeting," which usually turned into a fun afternoon where we discussed new strategies for expanding my brand.

"I'm just a bear," I joked, rolling my eyes as I took a sip of my drink.

"A very lucrative bear," she shot back, her eyes gleaming with mischief. "You've got quite the reputation now, Ciaran the Charmer."

***

Andie was not just my mentor; she was becoming something of a traveling companion. Since I'd been doing so well, she decided to treat me to little getaways across Europe. "You've earned it," she said, her smile bright as she revealed her latest plan. "We're going to Paris this weekend. I have a business event to attend, and you're coming with me as my boy toy."

The idea made my stomach flip with excitement. "Boy toy? I didn't realize that was my new title."

"Well, let's be honest—you're the perfect distraction," she said with a wink. "And it's not just for show; it helps me network, too."

The trip to Paris felt like a dream—one I wasn't quite sure I deserved. Andie had called it a business trip, but it quickly became clear that her real intention was to show me off like a prize.

"Pack light," she told me before we boarded the flight. "I'll take care of the rest."

Walking out of Charles de Gaulle airport, I felt myself being whisked into the world of wealth and privilege at a speed that left me breathless.

Andie's first stop wasn't the hotel, but to a high-end shopping district near Avenue Montaigne. I stood awkwardly in a boutique while a team of salespeople fussed over me, treating me like some kind of celebrity.

"He needs something sharp but not stiff," Andie instructed, her French smooth and confident. "Stylish, but... playful."

"Right, playful," I muttered, shifting my weight uncomfortably. I wasn't exactly used to clothes with price tags that made me nauseous.

The saleswoman handed me a navy blazer that felt as soft as silk between my fingers. Then came slim-fit dress pants, crisp white shirts, and a designer watch—things I never would have imagined owning in a million years. I marveled at how effortlessly Andie handed over her credit card for everything, her confidence making it seem completely normal.

As I tried on the clothes, I couldn't help but feel a rush of excitement. I was stepping into a new version of myself, one that felt bold and alive.

"You need to look the part," Andie said with a smirk, running her hand down my newly tailored sleeve. "We're not just here for fun, you know. I have appearances to keep up."

By the time we left the boutique, I looked like a model straight out of a magazine—my scruffy, laid-back demeanor transformed into something suave and polished.

"Now you're ready for Paris," Andie said, sliding her arm through mine and flashing me a satisfied grin.

While Andie was busy with her business meetings, she handed me an envelope stuffed with crisp euros.

"Have fun," she told me. "I want you to experience Paris. Buy yourself something nice. Get lost. Just be back by dinner."

I grinned, tucking the envelope into my blazer pocket. "You spoil me, you know."

Andie kissed me on the cheek, her perfume lingering in the air. "You've earned it, sweetheart."

With money to burn and no real agenda, I wandered through the streets of Paris like a kid in a candy store. I strolled along the Seine, marveling at the Gothic splendor of Notre Dame, feeling awed by the beauty that surrounded me. I treated myself to pastries from quaint patisseries, letting the sweet flavors melt on my tongue, and pretended to understand the art at the

Louvre, soaking in the grandeur of the place.

At lunchtime, I settled at a sidewalk café, sipping espresso and watching the world go by. For the first time in my life, I felt truly at ease, reveling in the energy of the city and the freedom of the moment. Everything felt bright and full of possibility, as if this was the start of something new and exciting.

The evenings, however, belonged to Andie. Each night, she dressed me in yet another flawless outfit—tailored suits, polished shoes, the works. We dined at Michelin-starred restaurants where I could barely pronounce the items on the menu.

"Just let me order for you," she teased one night, her hand resting on my knee under the table.

I was grateful for it; I'd never eaten food this fancy before, and my attempts at French were less than stellar. But Andie carried us effortlessly through the night, charming everyone from waiters to business associates with her easy confidence.

After dinner, we strolled along the Champs-Élysées, her heels clicking on the cobblestones as I tried to keep up. Every glance and every touch from her felt electric, carrying a promise of what would unfold later behind the closed doors of our hotel suite.

Andie didn't just want sex from me—she wanted seduction—the kind that took time and effort. She knew how to wind me up throughout the day, whispering things into my ear, brushing her lips across my neck, or running her fingers teasingly along my thigh during long cab rides.

By the time we reached our suite each night, I was a tangled mess of nerves and desire. Andie had this incredible ability to unravel me, bit by bit, leaving me craving more of her with every encounter.

Our days in Paris had been filled with adventure and laughter, bursting with spontaneity I never imagined experiencing. We strolled along the Seine, exploring quaint cafés and vibrant art galleries, my heart racing, not just from the breathtaking sights but also from the exhilaration of being in such an elite circle. Andie knew how to flaunt her connections, and it was an intoxicating feeling to stand by her side, drawing the attention of those around us.

One evening, as we settled into the plush elegance of a luxurious Parisian hotel room, Andie handed me a glass of champagne. "Here," she said, her eyes sparkling with mischief. "Cheers to your success, my charming bear!"

I raised my glass, feeling a rush of pride that coursed through me. "To new adventures!"

We laughed and celebrated under the glow of the Eiffel Tower, a backdrop that felt almost magical. For that brief moment, the weight of my old life faded into a distant memory, replaced by the thrill of what lay ahead. I was living a life filled with unexpected twists, boundless fun, and the exhilarating realization that I was becoming someone new, someone Andie was proud of. It was a feeling I would never trade for anything, and it was just the beginning.

That night, in Paris, I sat on the edge of the bed, my dress slacks crumpled around my bare feet, watching Andie as she stood in front of the floor-to-ceiling windows. She gazed out at the glittering city, her sleek black dress clinging to her body like a second skin, exuding an air of confidence that made my heart race.

"Tonight," she said without looking back at me, "you're going to seduce me."

I blinked, caught off guard. "Uh… what?"

Andie turned, a demanding smile playing on her lips, her eyes sparkling with mischief. "You heard me. You've learned a lot during our time together, but now it's time for you to take control. I want to see what you've got."

I rubbed the back of my neck, feeling the pressure mounting. "No pressure, right?"

She began walking toward me, slowly unzipping her dress as she moved, her gaze locked onto mine with an intensity that left me breathless. "No pressure at all, Ciaran. Just… impress me."

The challenge in her voice sent a thrill through me. I knew this was my moment to rise to her demands, to show her that I could match her boldness. With every inch she revealed, my nerves ignited into a fiery determination.

I stood there, my heart racing and nerves churning in my stomach. This was more than just a playful challenge; I recognized it as a test, one that I was determined not to fail. Taking a deep breath, I stepped forward and gently slipped the dress off Andie's shoulders, my fingers trembling slightly, but I kept my movements deliberate and slow. The thrill coursing through me only heightened my focus.

"You've been teasing me all day," I murmured, letting my lips brush against her collarbone, feeling her shiver beneath my touch. "Now, it's my turn."

I could see the shift in her expression; Andie's breath hitched, her usual air of dominance melting away as my hands roamed over her body with newfound confidence. I kissed her neck and shoulders, savoring the way she leaned into each caress, a soft sigh escaping her lips.

Finally, I laid her down on the bed, taking my time as I enjoyed this moment just as much for myself as for her. Each kiss, each caress, was deliberate and filled with intention. I knew exactly what she craved, but I made her wait—just long enough to drive her wild with anticipation.

Andie's moans filled the room, a symphony of pleasure that only fueled my desire. I moved with a slow, deliberate rhythm, matching her every movement, our bodies perfectly in sync.

As the moment built to its peak, the intensity was electrifying. I could feel every pulse of her excitement, and it pushed me to go further, to explore every inch of her with the intimacy she demanded. When the moment finally came, it was explosive—both of us lost in the overwhelming sensation, tangled together in the soft sheets as the twinkling lights of Paris danced outside the window. In that blissful chaos, I realized that I had not only met her challenge but had also found a depth of connection that left me breathless.

"You've come a long way, haven't you?" she whispered, her voice soft yet full of warmth.

I grinned, pulling her closer. "I had a good teacher."

Andie laughed softly, brushing her lips against mine, her touch igniting a warmth within me. "I think you're ready to graduate."

In that moment, I couldn't help but feel a swell of pride. We lay in comfortable silence for a while, the weight of the evening settling around us like a warm blanket. For me, Paris would forever be etched in my memory—not just as the city of lights, but as the place where I learned.

We laid there on the plush, oversized bed in the high-end Parisian hotel, wrapped in the quiet stillness that only follows a night like that. The room was dimly lit, with just enough glow from the soft, amber bedside lamp casting warm shadows over everything. High-thread-count sheets, now tousled and tangled around us, were cool against my skin, a welcome contrast to the warmth we'd just shared.

Andie lay beside me, her chest rising and falling in slow, satisfied breaths. Her cheeks were flushed, and that giddy smile played on her lips as she gazed up at the ornate ceiling. Her hair, now loose from its ponytail, fanned out over the pillow like a golden halo, and her fingers lazily traced small circles on my arm. She turned her head and gave me a look that was both soft and playful, her eyes reflecting that sense of wonder and excitement I'd noticed in her before.

I took in the room around us—the rich, red velvet curtains drawn over the large windows, the old Parisian charm that made everything feel timeless, as if we were in a different world altogether. The faint hum of the city drifted up from the street below, but here, we were in our own bubble. It was luxurious, yes, but the elegance of it all felt incidental. It was the quiet intimacy, the sheer realness of just being together, that mattered most.

Andie laughed softly, almost to herself, as if marveling at the whole experience. "Paris," she whispered with a sigh, her voice tinged with a hint of disbelief, as if it was all a dream. I couldn't help but smile in return. The night had been unforgettable, and the weight of that reality wrapped around us as much as the sheets did. The moment felt perfect, fleeting, and I found myself just wanting to hold on to it, to her, for as long as I could.

Somehow, that felt like an achievement worth celebrating. Yet, amidst the excitement, a small voice in my head nagged at me, warning that it was all too good to be true. How long could this last? I found myself worrying about what would happen when my studies became overwhelming or if my clients lost interest. The weight of uncertainty pressed down on me, and I couldn't help but wonder if this was just a fleeting fantasy.

But as I sat there with Andie, watching her smile light up the room, my worries seemed to melt away, if only for a moment. The laughter we shared and the electric chemistry between us felt real, pulling me into a world where I could be free—free from the constraints of my previous expectations and the pressures of my everyday life. This was my chance to seize the day, to enjoy life fully.

"Just remember," Andie said, breaking into my thoughts with a tone that was both serious and caring, "this is a business. You need to keep your head clear. If it ever feels overwhelming, you come to me, alright?"

"Deal," I agreed, raising my glass once more, feeling a surge of gratitude for her understanding nature.

As I watched her, something began to shift within me. It was more than just the thrill of a new adventure or the excitement of our physical connection; I was starting to see her in a different light. My feelings for Andie were evolving, transcending the boundaries of mere attraction.

I could feel the shift in the air between Andie and me, too. It started subtly—those moments when she caught me staring a little too long or when I'd laugh at her jokes just a bit harder than necessary. I tried to play it cool, but deep down, I knew I was developing feelings for her. It wasn't just the chemistry we shared or the thrill of our arrangement; it was the way she looked at me, the way her smile lit up when I said something clever, and the warmth of her laughter that made my heart race.

For now, I was savoring every moment—every laugh, every thrilling adventure, and every intimate touch that sparked my heart. I felt my emotions deepen, transforming into something richer and more meaningful. It was no longer just about the chemistry; I began to realize how much I valued her companionship, her insight, and the way she made me feel alive. Each time we shared a quiet moment or burst into laughter, the warmth in my chest grew stronger, hinting at the possibility of something more than just a passionate connection.

As we toasted to our adventures, I couldn't help but wonder if I was ready to let go of my fears and embrace an unexpected romance with her. The thought filled me with hope and excitement, suggesting that perhaps this wasn't just a fleeting moment but the start of something truly beautiful.

One evening, as we lounged in the lavish hotel room, I couldn't help but feel overwhelmed by everything. Andie was beautiful, smart, and captivating. I admired her not just for her charm, but for the confidence she exuded. Yet, amid all this, a small voice in my head reminded me that we had established this arrangement for a reason.

"Ciaran," she said, breaking into my thoughts as

she leaned back against the plush pillows, her eyes sparkling with mischief. "You've been looking at me differently lately. It's almost like you're developing a crush."

I opened my mouth to protest, but she waved her hand dismissively. "Oh, don't deny it! It's cute, really," she teased, but I could sense the seriousness underlying her words. "But let's be clear here: this is strictly a business arrangement."

The weight of her statement sank in, and I felt a flush of embarrassment creep up my neck. I had let my emotions get the better of me, and now I was faced with the stark reality of our situation.

"You're a young man with a lot to offer, and I enjoy our time together," she continued, her tone shifting to something more earnest. "But I need you to understand that it's important to keep our boundaries. This is about fun and pleasure, not love."

I swallowed hard, my heart racing, not just from her words but from the truth of them. I wanted to argue, to convince her that what I felt was more than just infatuation, but I knew better than to cross that line. Andie was right; I had to keep my head clear.

"Trust me," she said, brushing a loose strand of hair behind her ear, her eyes locking onto mine. "You have plenty of time for love in your life. But for now, let's enjoy what we have and not complicate things with feelings."

Her gentle but firm reminder felt like a cold splash

of water, and I nodded, the acceptance of her words settling heavily in my chest. I raised my glass, trying to muster a smile, but the weight of her words lingered in the air between us. I was still drawn to her—no denying that. But I knew I had to tread carefully and keep my heart in check if I wanted to navigate this arrangement without losing myself completely.

As we toasted to our continued adventures, I felt a mix of disappointment and determination. I could enjoy our time together without falling too deeply, but I couldn't shake the feeling that letting her go would be harder than I anticipated.

Chapter 10

CHRISTMAS

Christmas was approaching fast, and for weeks I'd been looking forward to going back to Canada. The thought of Saskatoon blanketed in snow, the smell of Mom's gingerbread cookies baking in the oven, and my dad's terrible Christmas sweater made me ache for home. I'd been counting down the days, but now I was sitting across from Andie, feeling torn apart by what she was saying.

"You can't leave now, Ciaran," she said, leaning forward, her dark eyes catching mine. "The holidays are the busiest time for us. Women are lonely, vulnerable, and... generous." Her lips curved in a way that made my chest tighten, but it wasn't enough to quiet the guilt gnawing at me.

"Andie," I sighed, running a hand through my hair. "I promised my parents I'd come home. They've been looking forward to it for months. I can't just... not show up."

Her smile softened, but her tone was all business. "I understand that, but hear me out. I've already got three clients lined up for you—women who specifically asked for you. All of them want someone to spend time with over the holidays. One's a recently divorced exec, another's a gallery owner whose family is overseas, and the third… well, she's a widow who hasn't celebrated Christmas properly in years. They need you, Ciaran. And I promise, it'll be worth your while."

I felt my stomach twist. The money would be good—more than good—but what about my parents? They didn't care about my bank account. They cared about me being home, around the table, where we could laugh and argue and pretend for a few days that life wasn't so complicated.

The call to my parents was the hardest part. As my mom answered, I could hear the excitement in her voice, and it nearly broke me. "Ciaran! Oh, we can't wait to see you. The snow's just perfect this year. Your dad's already started setting up the lights!"

I forced a smile, even though she couldn't see it. "Hey, Mom. Listen, I've got... a lot of work to do over the holidays. I'm really sorry, but I can't make it home this year."

The silence that followed felt endless. Finally, she

said, "Oh. Well, I guess we understand. Your studies are important."

Her words were kind, but the disappointment in her voice was like a punch to the gut. I could hear my dad in the background, asking what was going on, and my mom's hushed explanation only made it worse.

When I hung up, I felt hollow. Guilt settled in my chest, heavy and unrelenting.

Andie was waiting when I returned to her office. "Tough call?" she asked, her voice soft.

"You could say that," I muttered, dropping into a chair.

She came around to sit on the desk in front of me, her skirt riding up just enough to be distracting. "Ciaran," she said, her voice low and smooth, "you're doing the right thing. And I promise I'll make it worth your while."

Her hand slid over mine, and there was a heat in her gaze that made my pulse race despite myself. Andie knew how to play me—how to make the guilt and doubt melt away, if only for a little while.

She leaned closer, her lips almost brushing my ear. "These women are going to adore you. They're not just paying for your time—they're paying for the way you make them feel. And you, my dear, have a gift."

I swallowed hard, trying to focus on anything but the way her voice sent a shiver down my spine. "I just... I hate letting my parents down."

"I know," she said, her tone softening again. "But

this is your life now. You're building something here, and it's okay to put yourself first for once. They'll understand."

I wasn't so sure about that, but as Andie laid out the details of the bookings, I felt myself leaning into the decision. The women sounded... intriguing, and the promise of making their holidays a little brighter did take some of the edge off my guilt.

By the time I left her office, I still felt torn, but the resolve was growing. This wasn't forever, I reminded myself. It was just one Christmas. One sacrifice for the life I was trying to build. My parents would have to understand—or at least, I hoped they would.

***

Christmas Eve wasn't at all how I imagined it would be. I'd pictured myself back in Saskatoon, sprawled on the couch with my parents, watching cheesy Christmas movies while my mom kept refilling the snack bowls. Instead, I found myself in Andie's high-rise flat, the city lights twinkling below like a sea of stars.

Her place was immaculate, of course—sleek modern furniture, polished floors, and a fireplace that wasn't really a fireplace but some fancy electric thing. It hummed in the background, casting a warm glow across the room. She'd gone all out, ordering a full turkey dinner with all the trimmings.

"Can't have Christmas Eve without turkey," she

said with a smirk, setting down plates that looked like they belonged in a Michelin-star restaurant.

As we ate, I couldn't help but ask, "What about your family? Do you ever spend Christmas with them?"

Her fork paused halfway to her mouth, her expression tightening for just a second before she shrugged it off. "I don't talk to them much. Haven't in years."

I waited, hoping she'd say more, but when she didn't, I tried a different approach. "What about... before? You know, before all this? Did you ever—"

"Fall in love?" she interrupted, her voice light, but her eyes betraying something heavier. "Once. A long time ago."

I leaned forward, curiosity piqued. "What happened?"

She smiled, but it didn't reach her eyes. "I chose my career. No regrets."

She said it with such finality, but I wasn't convinced. There was a flicker in her gaze, a shadow that suggested she'd replayed that decision more times than she'd admit.

"I don't believe you," I said softly.

Her laugh was short and sharp, a deflection more than anything. "Believe what you want, darling. What's done is done."

We let it drop after that, moving on to lighter topics. She poured us each a generous glass of wine, and before I knew it, we were sprawled on the couch. Dolly Parton's Christmas album played in the background. Andie knew all the words. Her voice was surprisingly soft as she sang along.

By the time "Hard Candy Christmas" rolled around, the wine had gone to my head, and I was feeling more at ease than I had in weeks. It was easy to forget about the world outside when I was with Andie, even if there was always this edge to her—a sense that she was holding back, keeping parts of herself locked away.

When the album ended, I stretched and yawned, thinking we were about to call it a night. But Andie disappeared into her room without a word, leaving me alone on the couch. I stared out at the city, wondering what Saskatoon looked like under the moonlight, when I heard her voice behind me.

"Merry Christmas, Ciaran."

I turned, and my breath caught. She was standing in the doorway, framed by the soft light spilling from her bedroom. She wore a deep red lingerie set that left little to the imagination—delicate lace, sheer panels, and a playful Santa hat tilted just slightly.

"Andie," I managed, my voice catching in my throat.

Her lips curved into a slow, knowing smile as she sauntered over, her heels clicking softly on the polished floor. "Don't look so shocked. It's Christmas Eve. I thought we could make it... memorable."

She stopped in front of me, her hands resting on

her hips. "What do you say, darling? Care to unwrap your present?"

As I stood there, dumbfounded and utterly captivated, Andie's figure seemed to blur the edges of the room, commanding all my attention. Her silhouette was bathed in the soft golden glow of the flat's recessed lights, every curve accentuated by the crimson lace and sheer fabric of her lingerie. It clung to her like it was made for her alone, teasing just enough to leave my mind reeling with desire.

Her gaze was the real undoing. Those sharp, calculating eyes I'd come to know so well were transformed, softened by something raw, yet sharpened by an undeniable hunger. Passion radiated from her, but there was something deeper—a fire in her that made the air between us electric.

She moved toward me with deliberate, measured steps, her bare legs catching the light, her hips swaying with a confidence that was almost hypnotic. Every motion was unhurried, like she knew I couldn't look away even if I tried.

"Ciaran," she said, her voice a low, sultry whisper, my name rolling off her tongue like a secret she'd been keeping all night.

I couldn't reply. My throat was dry, my heart pounding in my chest so loudly I swore she could hear it. She reached out, her manicured fingers trailing along my jawline, tilting my face up just enough to meet her eyes. The intensity there was staggering—

like she was seeing straight through me, reading every thought, every flicker of hesitation, and answering it with a silent, *I dare you.*

"Do you know what you do to me?" she murmured, her voice thick with emotion and desire.

I swallowed hard, unable to find words. Her lips curved into a small, knowing smile—one that was equal parts invitation and challenge.

When she closed the final inches between us, her hands slid up my chest, the heat of her touch searing through the fabric of my shirt. She pressed against me, her body fitting against mine like we were two pieces of a puzzle, and my hands instinctively found her waist. Her skin beneath the delicate lace was warm and soft, and I was hit with the faintest trace of her perfume—something heady and floral, mixed with the natural warmth of her.

Her breath brushed against my neck as she leaned in, her lips grazing my ear. "You've been driving me crazy," she whispered, and I felt the shiver it sent through me ripple straight to my core.

The restraint I'd been clinging to snapped like a taut wire. I kissed her, hard, fueled by the same wild energy I saw mirrored in her eyes. She responded instantly, her fingers tangling in my hair, pulling me closer like she couldn't bear the space between us.

There was no hesitation, no second-guessing. Everything about her—the way she moved, the way she touched me—was charged with urgency, but also something deeper, more primal. She wasn't just kissing me; she was consuming me, making it clear that for this moment, I was hers.

When we finally broke apart, gasping for breath, she rested her forehead against mine, her fingers tracing the line of my jaw. Her lips were swollen, her cheeks flushed, and the fire in her eyes hadn't dimmed one bit.

"Don't hold back, Ciaran," she said softly, her voice trembling with the weight of her desire. "Not tonight."

And in that instant, nothing else mattered—not the questions, not the guilt, not the world outside her posh London flat. It was just her, just us, and the undeniable pull that neither of us could resist.

I woke up on Christmas morning with Andie nestled in my arms, her back pressed against my chest. The soft light of dawn filtered through the curtains of her posh flat, casting a golden glow on the room. For a moment, I lay there, content. Her hair tickled my face, and I could feel her steady breathing, her warmth grounding me in a way I hadn't expected. I couldn't remember the last time Christmas morning felt this peaceful, this...right.

But then she shifted, carefully extricating herself from my embrace. I opened my eyes to see her sitting on the edge of the bed, her back to me. There was something guarded in the way she held herself, her shoulders tense as if she were bracing for something.

"Merry Christmas," I said softly, propping myself

up on one elbow.

She turned her head, offering me a faint smile, but it didn't reach her eyes. "Merry Christmas, Ciaran."

It wasn't like her to be distant, not after last night. I wanted to ask her what was wrong, but I held back. Andie was a puzzle—always giving just enough but never too much.

Instead, she stood and walked to a sleek wardrobe in the corner, pulling out a neatly wrapped box. "Here," she said, placing it on the bed beside me. "Merry Christmas."

I sat up fully, the cool air of the room brushing against my skin as I reached for the box. It was heavier than I expected. I tore off the wrapping paper to reveal an expensive leather jacket. The kind of jacket I'd always admired but could never justify buying.

"Andie…this is…" I trailed off, running my hand over the buttery-soft leather. "It's amazing. Thank you."

She shrugged, her tone breezy. "You needed something nicer. Consider it an investment in your image."

I laughed softly, but her words stung a little. An investment. Always professional, even on Christmas morning.

"You didn't have to," I said, watching her carefully. "But thank you. Really."

She nodded, avoiding my gaze. "You're welcome."

I sat there for a moment, holding the jacket, before

glancing up at her. "Let me take you out for breakfast. My treat. It's Christmas, after all."

Andie hesitated, smoothing down the silk robe she'd thrown on. "I can't," she said finally. "I have a flight to catch."

"A flight?" I frowned. "On Christmas Day?"

She nodded, her eyes darting to the window. "Work stuff. You know how it is."

I didn't believe her. Something in her tone didn't sit right, but I didn't press. Andie was fiercely private, and I knew better than to push her.

"Well, safe travels then," I said, forcing a smile.

She leaned over and kissed me lightly on the cheek before standing. "You should head back. I'm going to start getting ready."

I dressed quickly, slipping on the new jacket, and left her flat feeling more confused than anything. The high from the night before had evaporated, leaving me with a nagging sense of unease.

Back at my flat, I collapsed onto my bed, the city unusually quiet outside. I grabbed my laptop, intending to distract myself, when I noticed a new email in my inbox.

It was from Shannon. Shannon Ryan.

My heart skipped a beat. I hadn't thought of her since I left Saskatoon.

Her email was cheerful, catching me up on life back home. She wrote about the snow, the cold, the familiar things I realized I missed more than I thought.

I typed out a reply, telling her about London—the classes, the city, the people. I left out the part about Andie and, of course, my…side job. Instead, I focused on the excitement of living abroad, the way the city buzzed with life, even in the dead of winter.

As I hit send, a small smile crept onto my face. Talking to Shannon felt easy, natural, like slipping on an old pair of shoes. And after the morning I'd had, it was exactly what I needed.

Chapter 11

DECEPTION

The first time I called Crystal, I sensed she was waiting for this kind of opportunity, but she kept her tone brisk. Her voice held a blend of curiosity and control, almost as if she was reminding herself that this was her choice, her adventure. We arranged to meet that coming Wednesday, midday when her house would be empty, a time she chose with precision.

When I arrived at her place, it was a quiet suburban home, well-kept but with a certain emptiness about it. Crystal greeted me at the door with an easy confidence that softened as I walked in. She wore casual clothes, but it was clear she had put effort into her appearance—her hair was perfectly styled, makeup understated but deliberate. I noticed the faint scent of wine as she led me through the entryway, and I caught glimpses of family photos on the walls—two kids smiling at the camera, a man who seemed to be her husband in several frames. I could feel a tension in the air, a slight nervousness on her end.

Crystal caught me looking at the photos and offered a quick, pre-emptive explanation. "My husband and I are… separated," she said, as if she'd rehearsed it. There was something hollow in her tone, as if the words were more for her own assurance than mine.

From then on, we fell into a rhythm that Crystal was very careful to maintain. I would come by during that same window every Wednesday, slipping in after her kids left for school and leaving just as promptly before they returned. Crystal insisted on it, making it clear how important it was that her kids never knew about our arrangement. She kept our time together casual on the surface, but I knew it was her escape—an outlet from what had become a dull, confined routine of day-drinking and isolation.

Every week, we shared hours that felt secretive, but the thrill for her seemed to build rather than fade. I watched her relax over the weeks, laughing more easily, letting her guard down with small admissions of her own. She was deeply guarded about her home life, though, giving me only glimpses—a brief comment about her kids, an offhand remark about the things "her husband never understood."

Crystal's insistence on timing was meticulous. Every detail had to be perfectly aligned; she'd watch the clock, reminding me of her rules with a subtle firmness that seemed to echo an underlying fear. She never put it into words, but I could tell she'd built walls around her choices, determined to preserve this secret life and keep it from encroaching on the other parts of her world. To her, it was a controlled rebellion, a carefully contained adventure that she could indulge without consequence, as long as I stuck to her terms.

For a month, we carried on like this, seeing each other with a kind of regularity that almost felt scheduled—her personal interlude, carved out from the responsibilities and restrictions that defined her every other day. And as much as I knew I was a small part of her escape, I couldn't ignore the feeling that what she was really looking for was much larger: a chance to remind herself of who she was before the routines, before the family portraits, before she ever needed an escape at all.

A week or so into the arrangement with Crystal, I couldn't shake the feeling that something was off. She was too precise, too strict about the timing, like she had a lot more to lose than she let on. The family photos, the reluctance to mention her husband except for those few vague comments—it all started to weigh on me.

So, I called Andie.

"Andie," I started, "what do you know about

Crystal's… situation?"

There was a slight pause on her end, a muffled exhale that I'd come to recognize as her way of choosing her words. "What do you mean?" she asked, her voice light, almost teasing.

"Andie, you know what I mean," I said, trying to keep the irritation out of my tone. "Is she married? I get the sense there's a lot she's not telling me."

She laughed, a little too easily. "Ciaran, love, Crystal is a grown woman. She knows what she wants, and she's making her own choices."

"That's not what I asked," I pressed. "Did she tell you she was married?"

Another pause. Then, in her typical roundabout way, Andie replied, "She mentioned… someone. But it's not like she's in some perfect, happy situation. They're not together; she's looking for a break, a little adventure. It's complicated."

Complicated. That word could mean anything. I could almost see her shrugging, brushing it off like it was all just part of the game. "Andie, if she's married, I don't want to keep doing this."

She sighed, and for a moment, her voice lost its playful edge. "Ciaran, I didn't think you'd get hung up on something like this. Look, people seek out these things for all kinds of reasons. Who are we to judge?"

But I couldn't let it go, and I decided it was time to ask Crystal directly.

The following Wednesday, I arrived at her place

as usual, but this time with a much different purpose. Crystal sensed the shift in me the second I walked in. She closed the door, her eyes darting to the clock, the same as always, but I didn't take my jacket off.

"Are you married, Crystal?" I asked, without preamble.

Her face fell slightly, a flicker of discomfort crossing her expression before she forced a laugh. "I told you. We're separated. It's… complicated."

"Separated, but still living here with your kids, with his picture on the wall? Crystal, you've been dodging this since we met. It doesn't add up."

She bit her lip, her confident demeanor softening. "Ciaran, it's not… that simple," she said, but I could see the struggle in her eyes. "My husband… he works a lot. He's hardly ever here."

I shook my head, the disappointment settling in. "Crystal, this isn't what I signed up for. If you're still married—if he's still a part of your life like that—I can't be part of this."

For a moment, she didn't respond. Her gaze lowered, and her shoulders slumped. "I just… I just wanted to feel something again. Something exciting."

I could hear the sadness in her voice, the desperation she was trying so hard to mask, but I knew my decision was made. "I get it. But you should figure this out for yourself before bringing someone else into it."

Crystal's face twisted slightly, and I could see she was trying to hold back a mix of emotions—hurt, anger, maybe a little shame. But she only nodded, looking away as I walked out. I didn't feel the thrill of an escape or the thrill of doing the right thing; there was just the hollow feeling of disappointment as I walked back into the bright afternoon, wondering why Andie thought this would be the right match for me.

As I stepped off Crystal's porch and into the driveway, I heard the rumble of a car engine and turned to see an older sedan pulling in, tires grinding against the gravel. A man stepped out—a little heavier, his face lined with exhaustion, a bit of hair clinging stubbornly to the top of his head. He looked worn, the kind of weariness that goes beyond physical tiredness. He saw me, and his eyes darkened as he took a few slow steps forward, his gaze flicking from me to the front door.

"What're you doing here?" he asked, his voice low but steady, the question hanging heavy in the late afternoon air.

I didn't bother with an excuse. "I'm here because of your wife," I said, meeting his gaze. His face twisted, and a flash of anger sparked in his eyes. I braced myself as he took a step closer, his fists clenching at his sides.

"You've been with her," he stated, voice trembling between a question and a declaration.

"Yes," I said, straightforward. "I thought you two were separated. She told me you weren't together anymore." The tension between us was thick, an emotional minefield, but I knew lying would only make it worse.

He took a swing, exactly as I'd expected. He was faster than I anticipated, and I only just dodged the punch, instinctively grabbing his arm, pulling him in, and locking him into a tight hold. I held him steady, feeling his struggle as he tried to push me off, his frustration bubbling over.

"Listen," I said, tightening my grip just enough to keep him from trying again. "I'm not your enemy, alright? I didn't mean for any of this to happen. She said you were separated. If I'd known you were still in the picture, I would never have been here."

His struggles slowed, his breaths coming in ragged gasps as he took in my words. His body sagged a little in my grip, and before I knew it, he was shaking, his shoulders trembling with barely contained sobs. A man who had once carried himself with confidence now crumbling under the weight of betrayal.

Crystal had stepped outside, her face pale, her hand covering her mouth. She didn't try to come closer; she just stood there, watching the man she had hurt. I never stopped to think about the consequences of this game and I never wanted to hurt anyone. I always saw myself as providing a service of sorts. A mutually benefitting arrangement between consenting adults. But this, this was not something I wanted to be a part of.

I let go of him, and he staggered back, taking a

shaky breath as he turned to face her. His expression was one of pure devastation, his eyes full of questions that he couldn't put into words. He looked at her for a long moment, and then something in him seemed to break.

He didn't say a word to her. Instead, he brushed past her, walked inside, and shut the door. I stayed, watching as Crystal stood there, arms wrapped around herself, her face streaked with silent tears. I could see the conflict in her expression—the regret, the shame.

A moment later, I heard a window creak open, and clothes began to fall one by one onto the grass, scattering around her feet. Crystal didn't move, just stood there in the dusk, alone and barefoot in an oversized T-shirt, watching her life fall apart. And as I turned to walk away, I couldn't shake the hollowness that settled over me, realizing that some things couldn't be unbroken.

I stormed over to Andie's place, ready to confront her. Setting me up with a married woman wasn't just careless—it was reckless. As soon as she opened the door, I couldn't keep it in any longer. "What were you thinking, Andie? Crystal's married. I don't need that kind of chaos."

Andie crossed her arms, looking unfazed. "Ciaran, she's a grown woman," she replied, meeting my glare without a hint of apology. "If it hadn't been you, it would've been someone else."

Her calm response only stoked my frustration.

"That's not the point," I said sharply. "This blew up in my face. Her husband was there, and you didn't think to warn me?"

But instead of showing remorse, Andie just took a step closer, her eyes glinting with that mischievous spark she wore so well. "You're right," she said softly, almost too soft for how smug she looked. "Maybe I should have told you. Or maybe... you're just angry because you feel caught up in something beyond your control."

I let out a rough laugh, but she only continued, inching even closer. "What's the matter, Ciaran? Afraid you didn't have a choice?"

The edge in her tone lit something in me, transforming my anger into something darker, something electric. I pulled her close, and she gave me that small, triumphant smirk, testing me. "You think you can push me around like this?" I murmured, tightening my hold. Andie's pulse quickened under my hand, and she met my gaze with that quiet, intense thrill in her eyes, her usual confidence fading into something more vulnerable.

"Maybe you're right," she whispered, her voice low, almost a dare. She was giving me control, letting me set the terms, and I could feel the thrill building as I held her there, finally in control of the situation. With every move, I could sense her holding back, waiting for me to take the lead. And as we drew closer, I could see she wasn't just playing—she wanted me to take charge.

A sultry glint appeared in Andie's eye, and her demeanor shifted. She stepped closer to me, her intention clear. I felt a stir of excitement and unease as she purred, "I always appreciated your creativity, Ciaran." I arched an eyebrow, curious and intrigued by the proposition I sensed lingering on her tongue.

"And what did you have in mind, Andie?" Her gaze fixed on me, intense and hungry.

"I think it's time you showed me just how creative you can be. I want you to dominate me, Ciaran." My heart raced as I imagined the possibilities.

I took a step towards her, my voice steady and full of promise. "I can be very persuasive when I want to be, Andie." I gently took her hand and pulled her closer, our bodies almost touching. "I think I deserve it," she whispered, her breath hot on my skin. I took control, my desire fueling my actions. I pushed her against the wall, my body pressing into hers. I wanted to show her the power she had ignited within me, the fire that had been smoldering since the moment I met her. My hands moved to her wrists, pinning them above her head as I leaned in, my lips brushing against her ear. "You asked for this, Andie. Now, I'm in control." Her breath quickened, and a soft moan escaped her lips. I wanted to tease her, to build the anticipation. Slowly, I trailed kisses along her jawline, down her neck, savoring the taste of her skin. My hands moved to the buttons of her blouse, slowly undoing each one, exposing her inch by inch.

"I think I'd like that very much."

Chapter 12

COMFORT IN GRIEF

As the leaves began to bud and the air warmed in early spring, I found myself heading into another unexpected chapter of my escorting career. Business was booming, and I was discovering that each client brought with them a new story—a new layer of humanity.

This time, I was set to meet Sheena, a woman who had recently lost her husband. The first time Andie mentioned her, she spoke in hushed tones, acknowledging the delicate nature of her situation. "Sheena is looking for companionship, but be prepared; this won't be your usual gig," Andie advised. "She needs someone to help her through her grief."

I felt a knot form in my stomach, a mix of

trepidation and curiosity. I had navigated the bizarre requests before, but this one felt different.

When I arrived at her apartment, the first thing that struck me was the air of quiet melancholy that hung in the space. The décor was elegant yet understated, with photographs of a smiling couple framed on the walls. A grand piano sat in one corner, its keys covered in a fine layer of dust. It felt like a shrine to what once was.

Sheena opened the door, and my breath caught in my throat. She was beautiful, with dark hair cascading around her shoulders and eyes that held a depth of sorrow. She wore a simple black dress that accentuated her figure but also conveyed a sense of mourning.

"Hi," she said softly, her voice barely above a whisper. "Thank you for coming."

"Of course," I replied, offering a warm smile. "I'm here for whatever you need."

She led me into the living room, where I could see an old pair of men's shoes neatly placed by the door, and a faded shirt draped over the back of a chair. My heart sank as I realized these were reminders of her husband—items she had kept close since his passing.

As we sat down together, the conversation started slowly. Sheena opened up about her husband, recounting stories of their life together, their love, and the void his absence had created. The more she spoke, the more I understood the complexity of her emotions.

"I just miss him so much," she confessed, her voice trembling. "It's like I can't let go, but I also feel so lonely."

I nodded, unsure of how to respond. "It's okay to feel that way," I said gently. "It's a part of the healing process."

After a while, she glanced over at the clothes hanging in the closet. "Would you… would you mind wearing his clothes?" she asked hesitantly. "Just for a little while?"

The request was unexpected, but I could sense her need for connection—a way to bridge the gap between her past and present. "If that's what you need, I can do that," I replied, my heart racing as I agreed.

After a brief change, I returned, now dressed in her husband's clothes. The shirt was a little snug, and the slacks felt foreign against my body, but I could see a flicker of comfort in her eyes as I walked back into the room.

Sheena smiled for the first time, her expression softening as she looked at me. "You look… just like him," she murmured, her voice laced with a mix of nostalgia and sorrow.

We spent the session talking, reminiscing, and sharing moments that felt deeply intimate. As the days turned into weeks, I became a presence in her life—an outlet for her grief and loneliness.

Yet, despite our emotional connection, she struggled with the idea of crossing the line into something more intimate. "I can't," she would say, guilt evident in her eyes. "It feels too soon, too wrong."

***

The second time I met Sheena, the air in London was damp and cold, the kind of evening that makes the cobblestones glisten like polished glass under the streetlights. Her house, a stately Redstone tucked away on a quiet street in Kensington, stood like a warm beacon. I rang the doorbell, and within moments, she opened the door, wearing a deep green dress that matched her eyes and seemed to soften the lines of grief etched into her face.

"Ciaran," she said with a gentle smile. "Come in."

The living room was just as it had been the last time—tasteful, cozy, a few photographs of her late husband still prominently displayed. We sat on the couch, an arm's length apart, and fell into easy conversation.

She asked about my studies, and I gave her the usual—philosophy, history, composition, too much reading and too little sleep. Then, without quite meaning to, I veered into a rant about the monarchy, spurred by some offhand remark about the Queen's recent public engagement.

"It's outdated, isn't it? An entire system based on bloodlines. It should be merit-based. People should have to earn that kind of influence."

Sheena tilted her head, a half-smile playing on her lips. "I suppose you're right. But there's something about Queen Elizabeth. She's... comforting. Like a constant in a world that changes too fast."

"She's fine," I said, shrugging. "But the institution itself? A relic. A gilded cage, really."

Sheena laughed softly. "You're very passionate about this."

I couldn't tell if she was amused or just indulging me, but either way, the conversation flowed, touching on politics, literature, and the absurdity of modern celebrity culture. As the evening wound down, the air between us shifted, quieter, heavier.

"Ciaran," she said softly, "would you kiss me?"

Her voice was steady, but her eyes betrayed the storm underneath. I leaned in slowly, brushing her cheek with my hand before pressing my lips to hers. Sheena kissed me back, tentative at first, then deeper. When we finally pulled apart, she was crying.

"Why?" I asked gently, wiping away a tear with my thumb.

"I enjoyed it," she whispered. "I haven't felt anything like that since Dominic. And I feel... guilty. Like I'm betraying him."

"You're not," I said firmly. "You're allowed to feel this. To want this."

She nodded, exhaling shakily. "I'd like to see you again, if you'll come back."

I promised her I would and not just because she was paying me, but because this was the first time I felt like I was actually providing a service that transcended physical gratification.

The next time I saw Sheena, she greeted me at the

door in a wool coat, a scarf tied elegantly around her neck.

"I thought we might go for a walk," she said. "It's what Dominic and I used to do. We'd walk through the park for hours, talking about everything and nothing."

I nodded. "That sounds nice."

We strolled through Hyde Park, the crunch of leaves underfoot mingling with the distant hum of traffic. Sheena seemed lighter, more at ease, as if the act of walking helped her shed some of the weight she carried.

"Do you follow football?" she asked suddenly, catching me off guard.

"Not really. I know enough to pretend I do when someone asks."

She laughed, a sound that felt like sunlight breaking through clouds. "Dominic loved it. He supported Arsenal. I always thought he liked the drama more than the game itself. Do you know about relegation and promotion?"

I shook my head, and she launched into an explanation, her voice animated as she described how teams could rise and fall between leagues, how it kept things competitive.

"It's like life, really," she said. "Nothing is guaranteed. You have to earn your place."

I smiled. "You make it sound almost philosophical."

By the time we returned to her house, the sky had darkened, the streetlights casting golden halos on the pavement. Sheena hesitated at the door, her hand lingering on the knob before she turned to me.

"Would you like to come in?"

Inside, the warmth of the house enveloped us. We stood in the hallway, and I leaned in, kissing her softly. She responded, and the kiss deepened, a heady mix of longing and restraint. My hands rested lightly on her waist, her fingers brushing against my chest.

Then she pulled back, her breathing uneven. "Ciaran, I'm sorry. I'm not... quite ready yet."

"You don't have to apologize," I said, my voice low.

She looked up at me, her eyes filled with gratitude and something else—hope, maybe. "I feel like I will be soon. Will you come back in a few days?"

"Of course," I said. I felt as though the moment was cheapened when she handed me the envelope, an elephant-sized reminder that this was a transaction and nothing more.

"You know, I could come back, for free next time. I enjoy being with you," I offered.

Sheena smiled. "That is sweet Ciaran and I appreciate the offer, but in order for this to work for me, I cannot be invested emotionally. Does that make sense?"

"Of course," I replied. As I rode away on my Vespa, for the first time, I understood my place and I didn't feel great about it.

***

After several sessions together, I could sense a

shift in the air. Sheena began to let her guard down, her laughter becoming more frequent, the heaviness of her grief slowly lifting. One day, as we talked on the couch, she reached out to touch my arm, her fingers lingering a moment longer than necessary.

"I don't want to feel this way anymore," she confessed, tears pooling in her eyes. "I want to move on, but I don't know how."

"You don't have to rush it," I replied, my heart aching for her. "You can take your time, but it's okay to feel alive again."

A spark ignited in her eyes as she looked at me, and I could sense the desire for change building within her. "Can you help me?" she asked, her voice barely above a whisper. "Can you… seduce me?"

The request hung in the air like a promise. I nodded, feeling the gravity of the moment. "I would be honored to."

The atmosphere shifted as we moved closer, her vulnerability radiating warmth. I took my time, wrapping her in my embrace, letting the tension dissolve as I whispered sweet nothings in her ear. My hands found their way to her waist, pulling her closer as our breaths mingled in the dim light.

"I want you to feel everything," I murmured, my lips brushing against her neck, igniting her senses. She shivered under my touch, a soft sigh escaping her lips.

With each caress, I led her into a world where her husband's memory could coexist with the present—a world where she could reclaim her sexuality without shame. My hands explored her body, tracing the contours of her curves, igniting the spark that had long been dormant.

"Just breathe, Sheena," I whispered, watching her eyes flutter closed as I showered her with kisses. I wanted to make this moment one of healing, helping her to find solace in pleasure rather than guilt.

The air around us thickened with desire as I led her to the bedroom. I laid her down gently, my hands roaming over her skin, each touch awakening her from the numbness that had held her captive. I took my time, teasing and exploring, reveling in the way her body responded to my every move.

As our bodies entwined, I could feel the weight of her past lifting, the connection between us growing deeper with each kiss and caress. The world outside faded away, leaving just the two of us in that moment—a sanctuary from grief and loss.

When we finally succumbed to the passion that had built between us, it was a slow, sensual dance—a celebration of life and longing. With each movement, I could sense her surrender, her spirit awakening to the possibility of joy again.

Afterward, we lay entwined, her head resting against my chest. Sheena sighed contentedly, a look of peace washing over her. "Thank you," she whispered, her voice thick with emotion. "I didn't know I could feel this way again."

I smiled, running my fingers through her hair. "It's okay to move forward," I reassured her. "You deserve to feel alive and loved."

In that moment, I realized that my role was more than just an escort; I was a guide for those seeking solace, helping them navigate the complexities of their hearts.

As Sheena drifted off to sleep, I found comfort in knowing that I was making a difference in her life. And with that thought, I embraced the journey ahead, ready for whatever unexpected twists it would bring.

Chapter 13

SOMETHING TO LOOK FORWARD TO

With each passing month, my life in London grew into something I'd only ever daydreamed about back in Saskatoon. By now, I had a solid lineup of regular clients, and every encounter was meticulously planned to fit around my classes. The money was good—better than good, really. I was able to afford a flat in a quiet corner of the city, which felt worlds away from the shared rooms and cramped spaces other students complained about.

Between client appointments, I found myself with ample time to focus on my studies. For the first time, it felt like I had a real handle on things. No more late-night cramming or rushing through assignments.

With the flexible schedule, I actually managed to stay ahead in my courses, and it felt rewarding to see my hard work reflected in my grades.

When I wasn't studying or working, I still had enough cash to explore the city—taking weekend trips to museums or cafes, meeting up with classmates for drinks, and treating myself to meals that didn't come in plastic wrappers. This balance between my classes and my work gave me a rhythm, a lifestyle, that felt sustainable and even fulfilling.

As spring came around, I decided it was time to pull back. I'd been running on high energy for months, and the idea of a summer break felt right. The moment felt bittersweet, but I knew it was what I needed. I called Andie and let her know that I'd be taking the summer off, so she could give my clients a heads-up.

Andie picked up on the first ring. "Hey, Ciaran! What's up?" Her voice was warm, but there was a familiar edge to it, almost like she'd been waiting for me to reach out.

"I wanted to give you a heads-up," I started, keeping my tone light. "I'm taking the summer off. Heading home for a few months to recharge."

There was a pause. "Heading home? So... back to Canada?"

"Yeah," I replied, smiling a little. "Time to catch up with family, see some friends—just take a break."

She let out a breath, but it didn't sound like relief. "But Ciaran, we have a good thing here. You've built up a solid base, and taking off for that long… clients will go looking elsewhere. It's a competitive business."

"I get that," I said, trying to reassure her. "I'll pick things back up when I'm back in the fall. I just need this, Andie. I'll keep in touch while I'm away, but I won't be seeing clients."

Andie's tone sharpened, catching me off guard. "You're serious about this?" Her voice softened a bit, but the disappointment was clear. "I thought we were on the same page. This isn't just about the clients, Ciaran. I was hoping you'd be around this summer… for us to keep working together. I've got plans, and they need you in them."

I took a beat, sensing something more than just business in her words. "Andie, I get it. We've done good work together, and I appreciate everything you've helped me build here. I won't be gone forever. I just need this break. It'll make me sharper when I come back, I promise."

She was silent, but I could almost picture her biting her lip, probably considering some way to change my mind. Finally, she spoke, her tone more composed, but still with a touch of insistence. "I suppose… as long as you're back in the fall. Clients like consistency, Ciaran. They expect it."

"I'll be back, Andie. You have my word. Besides, I'll be in touch. This is just a breather, not a goodbye."

For a moment, I wondered if she'd push further, but then she exhaled, sounding half resigned, half satisfied. "Fine, take your 'breather.' But when you're back, don't expect the game to be the same. Clients have a way of moving on."

I smiled to myself. "We'll see. I think they'll miss me."

She laughed, but it was a little more clipped than usual. "Fine, go be a regular guy for a while. But don't forget—you and I have a good thing going."

With a sigh that seemed to signal an unspoken acceptance, Andie hung up, and I felt a sense of freedom wash over me. This summer was going to be about reconnecting with myself. But as I hung up the phone, I knew that London, and Andie, would be waiting when I got back.

Helping Sheena had shaken something loose in me. At first, I'd seen her like any other client—someone who needed companionship, a distraction from grief, a little tenderness in the wake of loss. But the experience had cut deeper than I expected. Sitting with her, talking, listening to her memories of her husband, and eventually holding her as she let herself feel again—it was intimate in a way that went beyond the physical. It left me craving something real, something lasting.

That craving lingered long after I left Sheena's house. For the first time, the walls I'd built around myself felt suffocating instead of protective. I'd gotten so used to keeping things transactional, to being what people needed without letting them get too close. But now, I wasn't sure I wanted to live behind those walls anymore.

It was around that time that my emails with Shannon had started to feel like a lifeline. She was doing her residency in Edmonton, Alberta, and her messages were full of stories about patients, long shifts at the hospital, and how she managed to escape to Jasper for skiing whenever she could. I could practically hear her voice in every word, bright and curious and full of life.

She was interested in London, too—more than interested. She wanted to know about the city, my classes, and how I was adjusting. I told her about the museums, the cafes, the way the city pulsed with energy even in the rain. I left out the parts about Andie and my work, of course, but even so, the connection felt genuine.

Our emails weren't just casual updates; they were long, thoughtful conversations. She'd ask questions that made me reflect on things I hadn't thought about in ages—what I wanted out of life, why I'd chosen London, how I spent my time when I wasn't studying. And I found myself asking her about her patients, her dreams, and what it was like to be so close to achieving her goal of becoming a doctor.

There was something grounding about her. While my life in London often felt like a whirlwind of late nights and blurred boundaries, Shannon's stories about her life in Edmonton were steadying. She had this way of talking about her patients that made me see the humanity in what she did—the long nights, the exhaustion, the occasional heartbreak. But there was also a fire in her, this unshakable drive to do good in the world.

I started to look forward to her emails more than anything else. Even when I was with clients, a part of my mind would wander to the inbox, wondering if she'd written back yet.

We talked about summer plans, and when she mentioned she'd be finishing her residency by then, I suggested meeting up back in Saskatoon. She jumped at the idea, and just like that, it became something I was counting down to—a chance to reconnect in person, to see if the ease we had in writing to each other would translate face-to-face.

For the first time in a while, I felt like I had something real to look forward to. Shannon's words reminded me of the version of myself I used to be, before London, before Andie, before everything got so complicated. Maybe this summer, I'd find a way to reconnect with that person—and with her.

Chapter 14

SUMMER TEMPTATIONS

Coming back home after a long year away at university felt like slipping into a favourite worn-in jacket. The moment I stepped off the bus, the familiar scents hit me first—the faint, salty tang from the river nearby, the earthy smell of damp sidewalks from a recent rain, and something else almost intangible, the smell of just... home. It was a mix of memories and familiarity that I hadn't even realized I missed until I was standing there, letting it all sink in.

I dropped my bag off at the house and decided to take a walk, tracing the routes I knew better than any campus path or London-street. The sidewalk led me past the park where I'd spent countless hours running laps and pushing myself through brutal workout circuits. The trails were just as I remembered, winding through the trees and stretching off toward the edge of the neighborhood. I couldn't resist grabbing my roller blades and hitting the trails. Gliding over the path, it all came back—the dips and rises, the tight turns around the trees. I'd skated these trails so many times, it felt almost automatic, like my muscles knew the rhythm even better than my mind did.

Eventually, my route brought me past my old jiu jitsu club, the sign a little faded but still welcoming. I stopped to watch for a minute, seeing people through the windows drilling moves on the mats, and it brought a strange sense of nostalgia. I could almost feel the coarse fabric of my old gi, remember the weight of a partner's hand on my shoulder, the struggle and strategy of each roll. I'd grown a lot since those days, but there was something grounding about seeing it again, like I'd reconnected with a part of myself I hadn't realized I was missing.

Being home brought it all back: the habits, the rhythms, the way everything just fit. It reminded me that no matter where I went or what I did, there'd always be these parts of me—these trails, this club, these familiar streets—that would be waiting, unchanged, and somehow that made all the difference.

My parents greeted me with warm hugs, their faces beaming with pride as they recounted tales of my achievements.

"Look at you, Ciaran!" my mother exclaimed, her eyes sparkling. "You're all grown up now!"

My father nodded in agreement, clapping me on the back. "You're going to do great things, son."

But beneath their proud smiles, I felt the familiar pressure of small-town expectations, coupled with a yearning for the adventures I had tasted in London.

One afternoon, I wandered into town to grab a coffee at the local café. As I entered, I was greeted by a wave of nostalgia—everything felt the same yet different. To my surprise, my high school fantasy, Ms. O'Neil, an alluring English teacher with the bright blue eyes and confident smile, was sitting at a table, grading papers.

I had always been attracted to her. Ms. O'Neil was one of those teachers you couldn't forget, even if you tried. She had this wild mane of curly brown hair that she styled with a blowout that looked straight out of an '80s fashion magazine. Her hair framed her face in a way that made her seem both fierce and friendly at the same time. She was thin, with an athletic look that hinted she could probably run circles around most of us if she wanted to. But it was her eyes that people noticed first, bright and sparkling, like she was always in on some inside joke. They made you feel seen, like she could sense exactly what was going through your mind even if you hadn't said a word.

Her smile was her signature—a big, narrow grin that could light up the whole room and make even the most bored students sit up and pay attention. Ms. O'Neil had this effortless charm, a combination of energy and elegance, that made her as unforgettable as her distinctive look. She was the embodiment of everything I desired—adventurous, educated, and just a bit unattainable.

"Ciaran!" she exclaimed, her face lighting up as she recognized me. "What a surprise! How are you?"

"I'm great! Just finished my first year at university," I replied, trying to sound casual.

"Really? That's fantastic! You must tell me all about it." She gestured for me to join her, and as I settled into the chair across from her, I could feel a familiar thrill sparking in the air.

As we chatted, I couldn't help but notice how stunning she looked; that hair, like a wave crashing around her, cascading in soft waves, her laugh brightening the mundane café atmosphere. The chemistry was undeniable, and I felt a surge of confidence I hadn't anticipated.

Over the next few days, our encounters became more frequent. Every time I visited the café, she was there, and our conversations grew increasingly flirtatious. I found myself drawn to her in a way I hadn't experienced before.

"Have you ever thought about coming back to school to teach?" she teased one afternoon, leaning forward, her eyes sparkling with mischief.

"Only if you promise to be my mentor, Ms. O'Neil,"

I shot back, my heart racing at the playful banter.

To my surprise, she didn't back away. Instead, she smiled coyly. "I could think of a few lessons to teach you. And, I think you're man enough to call me Ginette now." She said with a salty playfulness.

It was a daring moment, and I could feel the tension hanging between us. Her gaze held a lingering warmth, and I knew that the barrier of teacher and student had blurred in that instant.

One warm evening, I invited her over for a drink. My parents' were out with friends and wouldn't be back until late. I thought I'd take advantage of the alone time. My heart raced as I set the stage—soft music playing in the background, the porch adorned with fairy lights flickering like stars in the night.

As she arrived, wearing a green top and white summer skirt that accentuated her figure, I felt a mix of excitement and nervousness. The atmosphere was electric, and as we sipped our drinks, the conversation flowed effortlessly.

"Do you remember that time you assigned us to write a romantic poem?" I asked, my voice teasing.

"Oh, I remember," she laughed, her eyes dancing with mischief. "You wrote the most scandalous piece in the class!"

I leaned in closer, letting the moment linger. "I guess I've always had a flair for the dramatic."

With a few playful exchanges and lingering glances, we found ourselves caught in a whirlwind of desire. I could feel the tension rising, and before I knew it, we were inches apart, her breath mingling with mine.

"Ciaran," she whispered, her voice barely audible. "You're not a boy anymore."

I leaned in, capturing her lips with mine. The kiss ignited something fierce within me—passion, lust, and an irresistible attraction that had simmered for years.

The following weeks were a whirlwind of stolen moments and late-night rendezvous. But as our connection deepened, so did her infatuation. Ginette became increasingly obsessed, often showing up unannounced at my parents' house, her eyes gleaming with a mixture of longing and urgency.

"Ciaran, can we talk?" she would ask breathlessly. I could feel the heat of my parents' watchful eyes, silently judging the situation.

"Of course, Ginette," I'd reply, my voice laced with concern. "But maybe we should keep this... discreet?"

She'd nod, her expression a blend of desire and confusion. "I can't help it, Ciaran. There's just something about you."

Chapter 15

SHANNON

Shannon was finally coming into town. Despite my time spent with Ginette, I couldn't wait to see her. Shannon had always been captivating in a unique, understated way. Her curly red hair was her crown—a fiery, untamed halo that seemed to match her personality perfectly. It framed her face with an effortless vibrancy, accentuating her sharp features. She wore glasses, the kind that hinted at her intelligence without trying too hard, and they suited her perfectly. Behind them, her hazel eyes sparkled with a mix of warmth and determination, a combination that made her approachable yet unmistakably focused.

She carried herself with confidence, the kind that came from knowing exactly who she was and what she wanted. Shannon wasn't flashy, but she had a magnetic presence. Her fit physique was a testament to her discipline; she worked out regularly, whether it was yoga, running, or hitting the gym. It wasn't about vanity—exercise was just another way for her to channel her drive.

What stood out most about Shannon was her personality. She was task-oriented to a fault, the type of person who thrived on lists, schedules, and goals. Yet, she had a way of making you feel like you were the only thing that mattered when she talked to you. She was pleasant and engaging, quick with a genuine laugh or an insightful comment that showed she was truly listening.

Shannon had this uncanny ability to balance her ambition with a grounded kindness. She could be fiercely determined one moment—whether she was discussing a tough case from her residency or her plans for the future—and then completely disarm you with a lighthearted joke or a nostalgic story about her childhood. It was easy to see why patients trusted her. She was a force of nature wrapped in a layer of warmth and authenticity.

Shannon was everything I admired: smart, driven, and genuinely kind. I found myself instantly drawn to her, our conversation flowing seamlessly as we caught up on each other's lives. She told me about her studies, her dreams of becoming a scientist, and I regaled her with tales from London.

Our first date, though we didn't call it that at first, felt like picking up the threads of something old and forgotten, but somehow stronger than ever. Shannon and I had been close through most of our childhood, inseparable at times, but our falling out right before I left had left a scar on our relationship. We went our separate ways, both a little bruised and struggling to mend our wounds. But tonight, it was like the year had softened whatever had made us stubborn back then. We met up, no grand gestures, just tacos and beer at this local dive. Nothing fancy, yet it felt perfect.

Shannon had changed over the year, but only in the best ways. She had this calm confidence, the kind that school probably instills in people, and her laugh had only grown richer, more resonant. We talked about world affairs, about everything going on in the world, and it was like old times, except there was more to say now. I told her about wanting to be a writer, to make something of myself that would last beyond the mundane, and she shared her own dreams in medicine, to help people in a way that was real and tangible. We had different paths, but the same desire to make a difference, and it somehow made sense. With Shannon, it was easy to be myself, to talk about things that mattered. There was no guard up, no need to be anyone but me. And in her presence, everything seemed simple, like it was supposed to be just us.

As the evening went on, we circled back to the past, and our falling out came up like a slow tide. It was strange—neither of us really remembered what exactly had happened to break us apart, just that we'd walked away hurt and angry. But as we talked, I realized something I hadn't dared to admit back then, even to myself. I had loved her, and from what Shannon was saying, I wasn't the only one who'd felt that way. We'd been in love, both of us, but too afraid to show it.

There was a long pause between us, one of those heavy silences where the words seem to hang in the air before you dare to say them. I reached for her hand, and she looked up, her eyes shining with a warmth that went beyond friendship. In that moment, we both knew there was nothing left to keep us apart, no more hiding behind what could have been. And as we sat there, sharing that simple meal and laughing as if nothing had changed, I knew this was the start of something new and real, a second chance that had been waiting for both of us all along.

The more time I spent with Shannon, the more I realized how much I had missed her. She was responsible and ethical, a stark contrast to the whirlwind romance I had with Ginette. I found comfort in her laughter and intelligence, a refreshing change from the chaotic passion I had with my former teacher.

But as I started to develop feelings for Shannon, I felt the weight of my secret life pressing down on me. How could I explain my escapades with Andie, and now Ginette, and not to mention everyone else in between? Would she even understand?

As I tried to navigate my feelings for both Shannon and Ginette, I realized I was caught in an intricate dance—between the thrill of seduction and the warmth of genuine connection. Each moment spent with Ginette filled me with excitement, while my time with Shannon made me feel grounded and seen. And then, there was Andie…

"*Ciaran, you've got to make a choice*," I told myself one night, lying awake in bed as the summer breeze rustled the curtains. "*You can't keep juggling. It's only going to end in disaster.*"

Yet, as I drifted off to sleep, my thoughts were filled with these women in my life—one, an intoxicating whirlwind, one a sophisticated business woman who opened up my world and my bank account, and one who was a comforting embrace.

As the summer unfolded, I knew I had to figure out where my heart truly lay.

Chapter 16

JASPER

It was during one of our late-night chats, sprawled on her living room couch with a bottle of wine between us, that Shannon brought up the idea of Jasper. Her eyes lit up as she talked about it, the way they always did when she was excited about something.

"There's just something about it," she said, curling her legs beneath her. "The air smells different up there—cleaner, fresher, like the mountains are breathing with you. It's not like Banff, all crowded and commercial. Jasper's quieter, wilder. You can actually feel like you're part of nature, not just passing through it." She smiled then, a little wistfully. "It's my escape, you know? When everything gets too hectic, I just go there, hike a trail, or sit by the water and let it all fade away."

She looked at me, her face soft with anticipation. "I think you'd love it. We should go."

How could I say no to that? The way she described it, I could already feel the mountain breeze on my skin, smell the pines, and hear the rush of distant waterfalls.

The trip to Jasper felt like stepping into a dream. Shannon and I had always shared a sense of adventure, and the rugged majesty of the mountains gave us the perfect backdrop to rediscover that side of ourselves together. The towering peaks, snow-capped and defiant against the sky, seemed to challenge us as we hiked through winding trails carpeted with moss and wildflowers. The air was crisp and alive with the mingling scents of pine and earth, invigorating with every breath.

We saw wildlife everywhere—majestic elk grazing lazily near the trails, their antlers an intricate masterpiece of nature. Big horn sheep perched impossibly on rocky outcrops, watching us with a wary calm. There was a moment of pure magic when we stumbled upon a serene lake at dusk, its glassy surface reflecting the fiery hues of the setting sun, while a pair of loons called out across the water.

On the second day we went hiking through a densely wooded valley. We rounded a corner and froze. Just ahead of us, a grizzly bear with two cubs was ambling across the trail. My pulse thundered in my ears as the massive animal stopped, sniffing the air, its dark eyes scanning the surroundings. Shannon's hand tightened around mine, and I could feel her heart racing as much as mine.

We stayed still, rooted in a mix of fear and awe, careful not to make any sudden moves. The mother bear's presence was commanding, yet strangely calm. After what felt like an eternity, she turned her massive head, giving us a final glance before leading her cubs into the dense underbrush. We stood there for a long moment after they disappeared, the forest silent except for the sound of our breathing.

"That was... insane," Shannon whispered, her voice trembling with equal parts fear and exhilaration.

"It was incredible," I murmured back, pulling her into a tight embrace.

The adrenaline of the encounter carried through the rest of the day. We went white water rafting in the frothing rapids of the Athabasca River. Shannon laughed and screamed with joy as the icy spray drenched us. Later, we explored the park on horseback. The steady rhythm of the horses' hooves on the trail grounded us after the wildness of the morning.

That night, in the quiet of our cabin, the excitement and intensity of the day seemed to settle into something deeper. The soft glow of the fireplace bathed the room in golden light as Shannon and I sat together on the edge of the bed, her head resting on my shoulder. She looked up at me, her hazel eyes searching mine, and in that moment, everything felt so achingly perfect.

When we kissed, it wasn't rushed or frantic; it was tender and deliberate, a slow unraveling of all the emotions we'd kept tucked away for so long. Shannon's hands rested lightly on my chest, her touch sending a warmth through me that had nothing to do with the fire crackling nearby.

As we lay together, it felt like the world outside had faded away. There was nothing but us—the rhythm of her breathing, the way her curls framed her face, and the quiet, unspoken understanding that we were both exactly where we were meant to be. It wasn't about passion alone, though that was there too; it was about connection, the kind that went beyond words or physicality.

When Shannon whispered my name, her voice was soft and full of emotion, and I held her closer, feeling as though we'd crossed some invisible threshold. That night wasn't just about making love—it was about rediscovering each other, about finding something profound in the quiet moments shared under a blanket of stars in the shadow of the mountains. It was about love in its truest, most unguarded form.

Chapter 17
GINETTE

After that night I knew what I had with Shannon was beyond anything I'd felt before and I wanted to be with her. I mustered the courage to break things off with Ginette. It wasn't easy; she had swept into my life like a summer storm, full of passion and allure. But deep down, I knew that her obsession was not healthy, and it would be better to break things off like a band-aid.

Meeting Ginette for coffee to end things was something I'd planned out in my head a dozen times, but even then, I didn't really know how it would go. She was unpredictable at the best of times—intense, fiery, and impulsive. We'd been together for a while, but my feelings had changed, and with Shannon back in my life, things had become clear. I had to move forward with Shannon, and Ginette deserved honesty, even if I knew she'd take it hard. I had no idea how to start this conversation.

"So," I began, my voice cracking like the first awkward words of a class presentation.

Ginette arched an eyebrow. "So?"

I tried to focus on the tiny foam heart in my cappuccino, wishing it would give me the words I needed. "I think we need to talk about... us."

Her eyes narrowed slightly, but she didn't say anything. She just leaned back, waiting for me to elaborate, her patience like a noose tightening around my neck.

I cleared my throat. "I—uh—I don't think this is working anymore."

Her expression didn't falter. If anything, she looked amused, like I'd just said something adorably naïve. "Ciaran," she said, her voice low and smooth, "what exactly isn't working? Because from where I'm sitting, we have something very special."

Her words hit me like a cold splash of water. Special. For a moment, I felt trapped between what she was saying and what I knew in my heart: Shannon. Shannon with her wild laugh and unguarded honesty. Shannon who made me feel light instead of weighed down.

"I just..." I stumbled, trying to collect my thoughts. "I don't think this is fair to either of us."

Ginette's lips curled into a small, wry smile. "Fair? Ciaran, relationships aren't about fairness. They're about connection. Chemistry. And we have that in spades."

I felt my resolve crumbling under the weight of her confidence. "But I'm seeing someone else," I blurted, desperate to make her understand.

For a moment, her mask slipped, and something sharp flashed in her eyes. She set her cup down carefully, the clink of porcelain against wood startlingly loud. "Someone else," she repeated, as if the words themselves were foreign.

"Yes," I said, barely above a whisper. "Her name is Shannon, and..." I paused, not knowing how to finish the sentence.

Ginette's face softened, though her eyes were still sharp. "Ciaran," she said gently, reaching across the table to touch my hand, "you're young. You don't understand what you're throwing away. Shannon might be exciting, but she doesn't know you like I do. She hasn't been there for you like I have."

Her touch burned like guilt, but I didn't pull away. "That's not the point," I said, though my voice lacked conviction.

"Then what is the point?" Ginette pressed, her tone almost maternal now. "Do you think she'll wait for you when life gets hard? Do you think she'll understand you like I do? Ciaran, what we have is real. You just don't see it yet."

I wanted to argue, to tell her that what I felt for Shannon *was* real, that it was different, brighter. But the words wouldn't come. Instead, I stammered, "I just... I think we need some space."

Ginette tilted her head, studying me like I was a puzzle she couldn't quite solve. "Space," she repeated, and for a moment, I thought she might laugh. Instead, she sighed. "If that's what you need, fine. But I'm not going anywhere. When you're ready to talk—really talk—you know where to find me."

She gave my hand a final squeeze before standing, leaving her latte untouched. I sat there, staring at the table, feeling like I'd just lost a battle I hadn't even known I was fighting.

By the time I left the café, the guilt and confusion had twisted into a knot in my chest. I had tried to break free, but somehow Ginette still held the strings. And the worst part? She thought we were still together.

Chapter 18

BBQ

A few days after my break up with Ginette, my family decided to host a barbecue. The sun shone brightly, casting a warm glow over the backyard as the smell of grilled burgers wafted through the air. My parents were bustling around, setting up picnic tables, and I could hear the laughter of my siblings in the distance.

Shannon arrived just in time, her curly hair bouncing in the sunlight, wearing a simple sundress that suited her perfectly. My heart swelled as I watched her interact with my family, fitting right in with their warmth and humor.

"Ciaran! Come help me with the grill!" my father called, and I laughed, shaking my head.

Just as we were settling in, the atmosphere shifted. The sound of tires screeching on gravel echoed through the yard, and my heart sank.

"Who the heck is that?" my brother asked, peering around the corner.

As if on cue, Ginette burst through the gate, hair tousled, clutching a bottle of wine like a trophy. "Surprise!" she slurred, her cheeks flushed.

I felt my stomach drop. This was not the scene I wanted for my family barbecue.

"Ciaran! There you are!" she exclaimed, her voice ringing out like a foghorn. "I've been looking everywhere for you!"

Shannon's eyes widened in horror, and I could sense the tension rising. "Uh, hey, Ginette..." I said, trying to navigate the awkwardness.

"Did you miss me?" she said, swaying slightly as she took a step closer. The scent of cheap wine wafted off her, and I winced internally.

"Maybe you should sit down," I suggested, motioning toward a chair.

"I'm fine! I just wanted to see my favorite boy," she declared, her words slurring together as she reached out to grab my arm.

"Ciaran, who is this?" Shannon asked, her voice edged with concern, her eyes darting between me and Ginette.

"This is Ginette, my... former teacher," I mumbled, feeling heat rise to my cheeks.

"Former? Is that what we're calling it now?" Ginette shot back, her voice loud enough to draw the attention of my family.

The laughter and chatter of the barbecue came to a halt as my mother, sharp-eyed and perceptive, approached. "Is everything alright here?" she asked, sensing the tension.

"Of course! We were just catching up," I said, forcing a smile.

But Ginette had other plans. "Ciaran and I were in love! And now he's just throwing it all away!" she declared dramatically, throwing her hands up in exasperation.

"Ginette, maybe now is not the time," I whispered, my voice strained.

But she wasn't listening. "You all should know, he was mine first! And I'm not done yet!"

My mother stepped in, her voice calm yet firm. "I think it's time for you to leave, dear."

"Leave? You can't just throw me out! I'm not done with him!" Ginette protested, her eyes darting around in a drunken haze.

"You can't just ambush him at a family gathering, dear," my mother said, her tone even. "It's not respectful to him or to our family."

As Ginette continued to rant, Shannon's face turned crimson, and she muttered something about needing to step outside. I followed her, my heart pounding with embarrassment.

"Shannon, I'm so sorry," I said, my voice filled with regret.

"It's fine, Ciaran," she replied, though I could hear the hurt in her voice. "I just didn't expect… this."

I sighed, running a hand through my hair. "I didn't either. I thought she would handle it better."

"I think you need to talk to her," Shannon said gently. "It's not fair to either of you."

As Shannon walked away to gather her thoughts, I returned to the barbecue, where my mother was still calmly escorting Ginette to the gate. After a few tense minutes, she returned, and I could see the concern etched on her face.

"Mom, I—"

"Go talk to her," she said.

I approached Ginette, who had tears in her eyes and for the first time, I was able to put myself aside and realized that I was dealing with another human being who had emotions, expectations and was looking for love; all things that I wasn't able to give her. I asked Ginette if we could talk somewhere quiet. When we finally sat down, I took a deep breath, steadying myself to do this right.

"Ginette," I started, looking into her eyes, "I want you to know how much I've valued the time we had together. What we had—it meant a lot to me. You taught me things about life, about myself, that I might never have understood on my own." Her expression softened a bit, and I knew I'd gotten through to her.

"But," I went on, "it wouldn't be fair—to you, to me, and definitely not to Shannon—if we kept this going. I care about Shannon, and I need to give that a real chance. Staying with you, even as friends, would only complicate things for all of us. I don't want to hurt you, Ginette. But I also don't want to keep hurting myself by pretending I'm someone I'm not."

She looked away, her hands tightening into fists. I could tell she was hurt, and it's not like she was trying to not let it show. Her voice was low when she finally spoke. "So that's it?" she asked, and there was a flicker of something vulnerable, almost pleading, in her voice.

Before I could answer, she leaned across the table, took my face in her hands, and kissed me. There was a fierceness in it, a sort of desperation. For a second, I felt the familiar pull, that sense of the old spark between us. But something was missing. My mind wasn't there the way it had been before; my heart just wasn't in it.

When we pulled apart, she searched my face, like she was looking for any sign that I still wanted this, still wanted her. But I could tell by the look in her eyes that she already knew the answer. She sat back, defeated but composed, accepting it without saying a word.

Ginette nodded, her expression a mix of sadness and resolve. "I hope Shannon knows what she has," she murmured. Then, with a final glance, she stood up and walked away. Watching her go, I felt a weight lift—a mix of relief and a little sadness. But as hard as it was to face her, I knew it was the right choice.

As I returned to the barbecue, my mother approached me.

"Let me talk to you for a moment, Ciaran," she said, her voice gentle but firm.

We moved to a quieter corner of the yard, away from the remnants of the barbecue. "What happened back there?" she asked, her brow furrowing.

"I thought it was over, but then she showed up drunk and made a scene," I confessed, feeling a mix of frustration and sadness.

"Ciaran, you're a good boy, and you deserve someone who respects you and your choices," she said softly. "What do you want?"

"I want to find someone who I can share my life with, Mom," I admitted, my heart racing. "I thought I wanted Ginette, but she's not what I need."

"Love is about partnership," she replied thoughtfully. "It's not just excitement or attraction. It's about being there for one another through thick and thin."

I nodded, the weight of her words sinking in. "You're right. I want something real—something like what you and Dad have."

"Just be patient, Ciaran. The right person will come along," she assured me, placing a comforting hand on my shoulder. "You deserve happiness."

As the sun began to set, casting a golden hue over the backyard, I realized my heart was beginning to settle. Maybe this summer was about more than just the chaos of love; it was about finding the clarity I needed to move forward.

As I rejoined the party, I glanced at Shannon, who stood off to the side, watching the chaos unfold. Perhaps I was ready to explore this new path, one where love wasn't just a series of reckless decisions but a journey worth taking.

Chapter 19

ENDINGS AND NEW BEGINNINGS

Shannon and I had spent nearly every day together since the barbecue debacle. The awkwardness had melted away, replaced by something more profound—a connection that felt both exhilarating and terrifying. We had talked about her transferring to the same university in London as I was attending, and the prospect filled me with joy and dread all at once.

"I can't believe summer is almost over," Shannon said, gazing up at the sky. Her curly red hair danced in the light breeze as we sat side by side on the porch steps, swinging our feet over the edge.

"I know. I'll miss this place," I replied, trying to

keep my tone light. But the thought of leaving home—and the life I had been leading—gnawed at me.

"Are you sure you want to go back? I mean, I can move to London, and we could figure everything out together," she offered, her eyes bright with hope.

My heart raced at the idea. "I want that more than anything, Shannon, but I'm not sure how it'll work," I said, running a hand through my hair. "I've been… well, I've been doing some things in London that I don't think I can keep up if you're there."

Shannon tilted her head, concern etched on her face. "What do you mean? Like, your studies? You'll be fine!"

"No, it's more than that," I confessed, my voice dropping. I knew I couldn't keep doing what I was doing if I wanted to build a relationship with Shannon. But I wasn't ready to tell her that I was working as an escort. I didn't want her to lose what respect she had for me. But deep down, I knew I was lying to myself. I was afraid of losing her, but I was also afraid of losing my job and the lifestyle it provided. I thought about all the things I could do with the money I was making: the trips I could take, the expensive gifts I could buy for Shannon and my family. It was tempting, but it also made me feel guilty.

I couldn't keep living this double life, but I also couldn't give up the money and the thrill of being an escort. I was torn between my desire for a relationship with Shannon and my need for financial stability. I knew I had to make a choice, but I didn't want to lose either one.

The longer I kept this secret, the harder it became to tell Shannon the truth. I felt like a coward, hiding behind my lies instead of facing the consequences of my actions. Even so, I couldn't bring myself to tell her, to see the disappointment and disgust in her eyes. It was easier to just keep pretending, to keep living this lie.

But, I couldn't keep living with the guilt and the constant fear of being caught. Every time I saw Shannon, I was reminded of how much I was deceiving her. I was afraid that if she found out, she would leave me and I would lose the only person who made me feel truly happy. I was trapped in a vicious cycle, torn between my love for Shannon and my need for money. I knew I had to make a decision, but I couldn't bring myself to do it. I was stuck in a web of lies, and I didn't know if I would ever find my way out.

Her expression shifted from confusion to shock. "Are you a drug dealer?"

"Ha! No, nothing like that. But if you move with me, I won't keep my job. It's too time consuming and between that and school, there'd be no time for us. See, I've been living this… lavish lifestyle, but it's not who I want to be. And I don't want to hide things from you any longer."

I felt the weight of my words settle between us.

Shannon remained silent; her brow furrowed

as she processed the information. "Okay, so if not drugs… then what?"

Part of me wanted to just let her think I was selling drugs, but I didn't think that would go over well. Since I still couldn't tell her the whole truth, I improvised. "Just like… it's hard to explain. I just take jobs at weird hours and I can be gone for days at a time. If I quit it will be fine, because if we're living together then we can split rent, bills, groceries and all that, so I won't need the money. I enjoyed the freedom it gave me, but now I realize it's not sustainable, if I want to be with you."

She took a deep breath, looking out over the yard where my siblings played. "So, you'd just give it all up? The money, the trips, everything?"

I nodded, the weight of the decision heavy on my chest. "I think I have to. I want to be with you, Shannon. I want to build something real, and I can't do that while living that lifestyle." Even though I was not telling her the entire truth, I feel like I touched on the issue enough to explain how I was able to afford everything so far.

A smile slowly spread across her face, and relief washed over me. "I appreciate you being honest with me, Ciaran. Even though I'm not sure exactly what it was you were doing, I know it must've been tough to tell me."

"It was," I admitted, with a sense of warmth with a side of guilt creeping in. "But I'd rather be honest with you than risk losing what we have."

Shannon leaned closer, her eyes sparkling with determination. "Then let's do it! I'll transfer to your university, and we can figure it out together. We can support each other."

Chapter 20

THE COUNTDOWN TO LONDON

The rest of the summer, knowing Shannon and I were about to start our lives together in London, was unlike any I'd ever had. We were inseparable, and everything we did had this thrill running underneath it, like each day was leading to something big. We'd get up early and go for long runs around the lake, laughing as we tried to outpace each other and stealing quiet moments by the water to catch our breath, our conversations drifting toward all the things we wanted to do once we moved. Those runs turned into rollerblading through town, where she'd speed ahead, looking over her shoulder with a grin that made me want to chase her down, just to be close.

Afternoons were made for ice cream stops. She'd tease me into trying the weirdest flavors, and we'd laugh at each other's ridiculous reactions. We'd share cones, sitting close on benches, with her head on my shoulder, and every moment felt as if it was framed by some hidden countdown, but one we both welcomed.

And then there was the lake. We'd spend hours there, swimming until our arms were tired, drying off in the warm sun with our hands intertwined. She'd lean into me, and I'd wrap my arm around her, each of us quiet, just taking it in. Every day felt like a memory we were building together—small, perfect moments that made leaving easier, because I knew we were doing it together.

One night, we had decided to stay by the lake after sunset, watching the stars. She nestled closer as the air cooled, and I felt this pull—this certainty that this was the start of something real. When she looked up at me, I could tell she felt it too. We talked about London, about our future, about what living together would be like, and somewhere in all those words, the feeling was undeniable. We were falling in love, completely, and for once, I didn't feel a bit of hesitation.

By the time we packed up to move, that feeling was solid, rooted in those summer days. Shannon was my best friend, my partner, and now something so much more. Moving to London was no longer about escaping or finding myself; it was about creating a life together, and I couldn't wait to start.

As I pulled away from my childhood home for what felt like the last time, I felt a strange mix of sadness and excitement. The road to London stretched out before me, and with Shannon by my side, I was ready to embrace whatever lay ahead.

Just then, my phone rang. It was Andie.

I let it go to voice mail.

Chapter 21

BACK IN LONDON

Moving to London with Shannon felt like stepping into a whole new world—not just because we were moving in together, but because I was seeing the city through her eyes for the first time. Shannon's excitement was infectious. From the moment we landed, she was wide-eyed, taking in the noise, the lights, the sheer energy of it all. And here I was, grinning beside her, thrilled to be the one introducing her to it. It was as if London had become this big, endless adventure we were about to tackle side-by-side, and I couldn't imagine a better partner.

Our first few days were an absolute whirlwind. We'd barely unpacked, yet we were already hitting the streets, wandering through neighborhoods, and uncovering the spots I knew she'd love. I took her to Trafalgar Square, where she insisted on a hundred photos with the lions, laughing and teasing me to join. Seeing her marvel at everything—the architecture, the vibe, the street performers—felt like I was falling for the city all over again. But more than that, I was falling deeper for her. Every time she gasped at something or grabbed my hand, her excitement was like this electric charge that ran through me. She was living her dream, and I was right there in it with her.

One afternoon, we strolled along the Thames, and I surprised her with a trip on the London Eye. Watching her face light up as we rose above the city, seeing Big Ben and St. Paul's Cathedral stretching out below us, felt like the start of everything we'd been talking about back home. She leaned into me, and we stood in comfortable silence, gazing at the sprawling city. Shannon kept squeezing my hand, barely able to believe we were here, actually living this, and I just wanted to keep sharing these firsts with her.

Then there were our cozy nights in. We'd come back to our flat, sometimes exhausted from all the sightseeing, and just collapse on the couch with takeout and a movie. She'd curl up next to me, her head on my shoulder, and it felt like we'd always been doing this—like this was home. I'd glance at her every now and then, catching her smile or the way she'd tuck her hair behind her ear, and every time, I'd feel this surge of happiness I couldn't quite explain.

Every corner of the city became our playground. We'd grab coffee near Covent Garden, where I'd show her the hidden spots only locals knew, and then head to the museums, where I'd "teach" her about random paintings with absolutely zero expertise, making her laugh so hard she had to shush me. She'd drag me to street markets, and we'd try every weird food we found, all while planning which new neighborhoods we'd explore next.

London was new for her, but everything felt fresh to me, too. I realized that this wasn't just about moving to the city or starting university—it was about building a life... with Shannon. With every laugh, every late-night conversation, and every shared look, I knew that taking this step together was one of the best decisions I'd ever made.

"Just think of all the adventures we're going to have," she said, glancing up with a smile.

"Yeah," I replied, forcing a smile of my own, though my heart trembled with uncertainty. "Adventures."

As we both stepped into this new chapter, I could only hope that the decisions I had made in the past wouldn't destroy the chance for our love and happiness I so desperately sought. But for now, as we stood together in our tiny London apartment, the future felt bright and full of possibilities. And maybe, just maybe, love would be the greatest adventure of all. If only I could leave my past behind me, but as is often the case, the past was becoming increasingly impatient with my eagerness to move forward.

Just then, the phone rang, its shrill tone cutting through the quiet of the flat. I tensed, glancing toward Shannon, who was curled up on the couch with a book, oblivious for now. The sound felt louder than it should have, like the universe was amplifying it just to mess with me. I hesitated, staring at the phone as though it might explode if I touched it. Shannon's eyes flicked up from her book.

"Are you going to get that?" she asked casually.

I forced a smile and moved toward the phone, my heart hammering in my chest. "Yeah, I got it," I said, snatching the receiver.

"Hello?"

"Ciaran." Andie's voice was low and steady, but I could hear the edge in it. "When were you planning on letting me know you were back?"

I turned away from Shannon, lowering my voice. "Andie, I can't—"

"You can't what?" she cut in, her tone sharpening.

"I can't really talk right now," I hissed, glancing over my shoulder. Shannon was still reading, but her eyes flickered toward me now and then, her brow furrowing.

"Not now?" Andie repeated, her voice rising slightly. "When, then? You disappear for months, and now that you're back in London, you won't even pick up the phone? You owe me more than this, Ciaran."

"I can't do this right now," I said through gritted

teeth, and just as I was about to hang up, Shannon's voice startled me.

"Who is it?" she asked.

I froze. "Uh, just someone from... before," I mumbled, turning my back to her again.

"Ciaran, don't you dare hang up on me," Andie said, her voice cold and deliberate.

Before I could respond, I heard the floor creak behind me. My stomach dropped as Shannon walked over, her hand reaching for the phone.

"Shannon, wait—"

She took the receiver, her expression puzzled but calm. "Hello?"

There was a pause, and then Andie spoke, her voice soft but unmistakable. "Who am I speaking with?"

"This is Shannon. And you are?"

Another beat of silence, heavier this time. I could almost hear Andie collecting herself. "Andie," she finally said. "I'm an…. old friend of Ciaran's."

I grabbed the phone from Shannon's hand, my face burning. "Thanks, I'll take it from here," I said quickly, pressing the receiver to my ear and turning my back on her again.

"Andie, this isn't okay," I snapped under my breath.

"You didn't tell her, did you?" she said, her voice dripping with a mix of disappointment and anger. "God, Ciaran, you're such a coward."

"I'm not doing this right now," I said and hung up before she could say anything else.

When I turned back to Shannon, she was standing with her arms crossed, watching me intently. "Who was that?"

I rubbed the back of my neck, trying to appear nonchalant. "Just... someone I used to see a couple of times. She's a little clingy."

Shannon raised an eyebrow, her lips pressing into a thin line. "Clingy?"

"Yeah," I said quickly. "It was nothing serious, just someone who doesn't really get that it's over."

Shannon studied me for a moment, her expression unreadable. Then she shrugged, though her tone was cooler than before. "Well, you might want to be clearer with her next time. She sounded pretty invested."

I nodded, forcing a smile. "Yeah, I'll take care of it."

But as Shannon returned to her book, I knew this wasn't over—not with Andie, and maybe not even with Shannon. The walls I'd built around my past were starting to crack, and it was only a matter of time before everything came crashing down.

THE PAST CATCHING UP
WITH ME

Chatter, underscored by the occasional honking of taxis, was all we heard as Shannon and I weaved through the crowd, hand in hand, strolling down the busy streets. Everything felt electric, charged with a kind of energy that only London could pull off. The buildings seemed to glow under the golden streetlights, historic and modern all at once, casting long shadows and illuminating the damp pavement in a way that made the city feel timeless. There was something invigorating about the rhythm of it all: the bustling cafés spilling over with people, the smell of fresh bread from bakeries that hadn't yet closed up, and the faint scent of rain in the cool air.

We were headed toward our favorite café, a little spot tucked away on a side street, intimate and unassuming, but warm. I'd never have guessed that such a place would quickly feel like ours. As we walked, I glanced at Shannon beside me, her face lit with that quiet, radiant smile that always made me feel like I was right where I needed to be. Here, surrounded by the city's heartbeat, with Shannon's hand in mine, I felt hopeful—hopeful in a way that I hadn't felt in years.

As we turned a corner to our apartment, that hope was abruptly shattered. There, standing at the entrance with her arms crossed and a look of pure indignation, was Andie.

"Ciaran!" she shouted, her voice cutting through the bustling noise. The moment I laid eyes on her, my stomach dropped. I had been avoiding her calls since our last conversation hoping she would take the hint. Apparently, that wasn't happening.

"Uh-oh," I muttered, squeezing Shannon's hand a bit tighter as we approached.

Shannon raised an eyebrow, sensing the tension. "Who's that?"

"It's… uh, Andie. The woman who was on the phone the other night," I stammered, trying to keep my voice steady.

Andie strode over, her heels clicking sharply against the pavement, her gaze locked onto me. "You've been avoiding me, Ciaran."

I swallowed hard, my heart racing. "Andie, I—"

"Don't 'Andie' me! We had a deal." she insisted, her voice calm and calculated. "I thought we were in this together, and now you're just going to ditch me?"

Shannon's grip on my hand tightened, her expression shifting from curiosity to concern. "Ciaran, what's happening?"

I hesitated, glancing at Shannon, whose eyes searched mine for answers. "It's… it's complicated."

"Complicated?" Andie scoffed.

My chest tightened, panic rising like a tide. I felt Shannon stiffen beside me. I turned to her, my voice strained. "Shannon, can you—can you wait inside for a moment? Please?"

Shannon glanced between us, her expression hardening. "No, I think I'll wait out here," she said, her voice calm but firm. She fixed her gaze on Andie, her chin lifting slightly. "I hope you can find the closure you need. But then, you need to move on."

Andie's smile didn't waver. She let out a soft, amused laugh, tilting her head as though Shannon's words had been a harmless joke. "You've got a strong spirit," Andie said smoothly. "I like that."

Shannon didn't flinch. "I'm not joking."

Andie shrugged, her confidence radiating like a shield. "Noted," she said lightly, before turning her attention back to me. "We need to talk, Ciaran."

Shannon gave me a look—part concern, part frustration. "Fine," she said after a beat, her voice tight. "I'll give you privacy, but I'm not going far." She stepped back, crossing her arms and leaning against the building wall.

I turned to Andie, my heart pounding. "What are you doing here?" I hissed.

Andie smirked, stepping closer. "Oh, Ciaran, I'm just tying up loose ends. You've been avoiding me, and I think we both know why."

"Leave," I said, my voice low but trembling.

Her eyes gleamed, a predator scenting weakness. "Not so fast. You see, I've realized something—you're hiding your past from her. Aren't you?" She nodded toward Shannon without breaking her gaze. "That little dalliance we had, your work for me... You haven't told her any of it, have you?"

I swallowed hard, glancing at Shannon, who stood a few feet away, watching us intently. "This isn't your business anymore."

"Oh, but it is," Andie said, her voice soft but laced with steel. "You're trying to rewrite history, Ciaran, and I'm not inclined to let you. If you're too much of a coward to be honest with her, then here's the deal: you come back to work for me. You do what I say. And when I say 'work,' I think you know I'm including me in the arrangement."

I felt my stomach churn. "You can't do this," I said, my voice barely audible.

"Can't I?" she countered, raising an eyebrow. "You're the one who's given me all the power here, darling. Either you play along, or she gets the full story. Every. Last. Detail."

I stood there, frozen, every part of me screaming to run, to fight, to do anything but submit. And then, for the first time, something broke free inside me.

"No," I said, my voice firm and steady.

Andie blinked, her smirk faltering for a fraction of a second. "Excuse me?"

"I'm not going to be your puppet" I said, meeting her gaze head-on. "You don't own me, Andie. And I won't let you control me."

She opened her mouth to respond, but I turned away, walking straight to Shannon. Her eyes widened slightly as I approached, but she didn't move.

"Shannon," I said, my voice thick with emotion. "I need to tell you something."

Her eyes searched mine, and after a tense moment, she nodded. "Okay," she said softly.

I glanced over at Andie. She stood there, her confident mask slipping just enough to reveal a flash of something else—shock, maybe even anger.

For the first time, I felt like I had the upper hand. But as I looked into Shannon's eyes, I knew the hardest part was still ahead. It was time to face the truth, no matter what it cost me.

I took a deep breath, knowing I couldn't keep Shannon in the dark any longer. "I need to tell you the truth."

Chapter 23

THE TRUTH UNVEILED

With a pained look, I turned to face Shannon completely. "I used to work as an escort. That's how I was making money while I was in London."

Shannon's eyes widened, her surprise evident. "An escort?" she repeated, her voice barely above a whisper. "Like… for sex?"

"Yes, well, sometimes. Other times, no. But basically… yes," I admitted, feeling the weight of my words. "It was a way to pay for school and everything. I thought it was just temporary, but it turned into something bigger." Andie crossed her arms, leaning in slightly, as if waiting for Shannon to react negatively. But Shannon just stared at me, a whirlwind of emotions flickering across her face. After what felt like an eternity, she finally spoke.

"Ciaran, I'm not going to lie; I'm shocked. I had no idea. But... everyone has a history, right?" I nodded, my heart racing as I watched her process the information.

"I'm not proud of it, Shannon. I didn't want to hide it from you. I want to be with you, and I promised myself I would stop if we were serious."

Shannon took a moment, biting her lip as she considered her next words. "So, you're saying you gave it up? For me?"

"Yes. I want to build a life with you, and I can't do that while living in the shadows of my past."

A small smile broke through her initial shock, and I felt a wave of relief wash over me. "I appreciate your honesty, Ciaran. I'm willing to move forward with you, but I need you to promise me that you'll stick to your word and leave that part of your life behind."

"I promise," I said earnestly, reaching out to take her hands in mine.

"Good," Shannon replied, squeezing my hands.

Andie's face twisted with a mix of exasperation and something deeper, something raw and vulnerable she couldn't quite hide from me. She must have realized, from the way I was looking at her, that I'd finally given up trying to break through her walls, and I could see the impact in her eyes. For a moment, I almost reached out to her, seeing the cracks in that hardened, businesswoman mask she'd perfected over the years. It was like watching someone try to hold back a flood with only their bare hands—determined, desperate, but ultimately losing the fight.

She tried to keep it together, forcing a cool, indifferent expression, lips pressed tight, arms crossed defensively as if that would shield her from letting anything slip. But her emotions betrayed her; a flash of pain, maybe even regret, was written all over her face. She couldn't fool me, not anymore. I could see the struggle behind her eyes, the effort it took to maintain that icy composure while everything she was feeling simmered beneath the surface, threatening to spill over. In that moment, she looked like someone caught between what she thought she needed to be and who she actually was.

"It was entertaining for a time, but inevitably, all good things must reach a conclusion." Andie glanced at Shannon, offering a suspicious grin before speaking again with a mischievous tone. "Don't forget to tell her about the time you put on a teddy bear suit and serviced that deranged woman...Farewell, Ciarin."

And with that, Andie walked out of my life forever.

Shannon looked at me, eyes wide with a mix of shock and confusion, like she was still trying to process everything she'd just witnessed—Andie's outburst, my admission about the escort work. It must've felt like a rug had been pulled out from under her, and I could see her grappling with that. Her lips pressed together, almost like she didn't trust her voice. Finally, she said she needed to talk.

I nodded. "Let's go inside," and we stepped into the coffee shop. I could feel Shannon's gaze on me as we walked, like she was piecing together parts of me she hadn't known existed. Inside the café, we found a quiet corner, but even then, I could tell she was struggling to wrap her mind around what I'd just laid out for her.

"I want to know everything." She said with a seriousness that sent a chill down my spine.

"I'm going to need something stronger than a coffee."

Chapter 24

SET FREE

As I sat across from Shannon, I took a deep breath and prepared to reveal my deepest, darkest secret: my time as an escort. As I spoke, I could see the shock and disappointment in her eyes. Still, the more I opened up, the more I felt a sense of relief. At the same time, a nagging voice in my head told me I was making a huge mistake.

What if Shannon no longer wanted to be with me? What if she thought less of me? But I couldn't stop now; I had to tell her everything. It was almost as if I was being controlled by some outside force, pushing me to reveal all my secrets.

As the hours passed, I couldn't help but feel a sense of regret and shame wash over me. What had I done?

I couldn't help but wonder what consequences would come from my decisions. The inner conflict within me raged on, tearing me apart as I waited for Shannon's reaction. I knew I had made a mistake, but it was too late to turn back now. I could only hope that Shannon would still accept me for who I was, despite all my flaws and mishaps. I told her every little detail, laying my shame out for her to judge me, to decide whether I was worth her time and most importantly, her love.

When I was done, I gazed down at the table, waiting anxiously for her response. Avoiding her gaze, I anticipated her to walk away without a word. However, to my surprise, when I finally lifted my head, she was beaming at me with a heartfelt smile. I was touched by her genuine understanding and acceptance, rather than mockery or amusement at my vulnerability. Tenderly, she held my hand and looked into my eyes, uttering these words: "We all have a past. Whatever that past may be and as long as it stays in the past, then I want you to know I love you."

As I gazed with delight and appreciation, my heart was filled with joy and gratefulness for the kindness and affection she had shown me. After leaving some money on the table to settle the bill, we strolled home hand in hand once again, basking in the quietude of the moment and taking in the various scents, sights, and sounds around us. For a while, neither of us uttered a word, simply relishing in the present. Then, Shannon's eyes met mine, conveying a sense of connection and understanding.

"And, what about this teddy bear suit?" She said with a little smile.

The question hung in the air, and I felt my cheeks heat up as laughter erupted from her.

"I—uh, that was a client," I stammered, trying to keep a straight face, but failing miserably. "She had a unique fetish."

Shannon's laughter rang out, clear and joyful, cutting through the tension. "So, you've really been dressing up as a teddy bear for your clients?"

"Not just a teddy bear! It was a whole performance!" I insisted, feeling utterly ridiculous. "I had to alter the costume and everything!" Shannon chuckled, shaking her head in disbelief. "Only you, Ciaran. You always did have a knack for getting into absurd situations." Shannon leaned into me, her eyes sparkling with mirth. "I can't believe I'm dating a former teddy bear escort."

"I swear, I'm so much more than that!" I protested, laughing along with her.

"I'm also going to be a very accomplished writer and—"

"Oh, I'm sure that'll impress the teddy bear community," Shannon teased, nudging me playfully. "Oh, and you're going to be getting yourself tested before we have sex again," she added.

"Yeah... yeah, that seems fair," I replied embarrassingly.

As we stood there, laughing, I felt a weight lift off my shoulders. Yes, my past was unconventional and full of oddities, but standing with Shannon, I realized that love could survive even the quirkiest of histories. In that moment, I knew I was ready to embrace this new life. With Shannon at my side, I was excited to move forward—teddy bear suits and all.

ACKNOWLEDGMENTS

I would like to thank Fay Thompson, who helped bring a story in my head into a story on paper.

ABOUT THE AUTHOR

Patrick C Duffy is a happy husband and a proud father, who has lived all over Canada and travelled most of the world while serving with the Canadian Forces and now calls Saskatoon home.

This is his first book.